Lunch Swap Disaster

DON'T MISS THE REST OF THE
SIXTH-GRADE ALIENS SERIES!

Sixth-Grade Alien

I Shrank My Teacher

Missing — One Brain!

Lunch Swap Disaster

Sixth-Grade Alien

Lunch Swap Disaster

Previously titled
Peanut Butter Lover Boy

by BRUCE COVILLE

Illustrated by Glen Mullaly

ALADDIN

NEW YORK LONDON TORONTO SYDNEY NEW DELHI

ALADDIN

An imprint of Simon & Schuster Children's Publishing Division

1230 Avenue of the Americas, New York, New York 10020

This Aladdin paperback edition August 2020

Text copyright © 2000, 2020 by Bruce Coville

Previously published in 2000 as *Peanut Butter Lover Boy*

Illustrations copyright © 2020 by Glen Mullaly

Also available in an Aladdin hardcover edition.

All rights reserved, including the right of reproduction in whole or in part in any form.

ALADDIN and related logo are registered trademarks of Simon & Schuster, Inc.

For information about special discounts for bulk purchases, please contact Simon & Schuster Special Sales at 1-866-506-1949 or business@simonandschuster.com.

The Simon & Schuster Speakers Bureau can bring authors to your live event. For more information or to book an event contact the Simon & Schuster Speakers Bureau at 1-866-248-3049 or visit our website at www.simonspeakers.com.

Book designed by Tiara Iandiorio

The illustrations for this book were rendered in in a mix of traditional and digital media.

The text of this book was set in Noyh Book.

Manufactured in the United States of America 0620 OFF

2 4 6 8 10 9 7 5 3 1

Library of Congress Control Number 2020935826

ISBN 9781534464865 (hc)

ISBN 9781534464858 (pbk)

ISBN 9781534464872 (eBook)

CONTENTS

FOR ASHLEY GRAYSON,
DEALMAKER
EXTRAORDINAIRE

Lunch Swap Disaster

CHAPTER 1

[PLESKIT]
A LETTER HOME
(TRANSLATION)

FROM: Pleskit Meenom, on the emotionally dangerous Planet Earth

TO: Maktel Geebrit, on the relatively sane Planet Hevi-Hevi

Dear Maktel:

Sixth grade is beginning to wear me down. Not only do I have homework and social problems, but I have the issue of being the only kid from another planet in my classroom. Actually, the only kid from another planet on the planet, as far as we know. Not to mention the only kid who is purple, totally

1

hairless, and has a *sphen-gnut-ksher* growing out of the top of his head.

After the events you will find recorded here, it is clear that the suspicions you shared with me in your last letter are correct; someone *is* trying to sabotage the Fatherly One's work. Or maybe many someones. The Earthlings do not yet realize what hangs in the balance for them. The Fatherly One has agreed to let Tim and me release these stories in the hope that the books will help Earthlings feel more comfortable with our presence.

Please do not laugh too much when you read about what happened to me when I was subjected to the amazing effect of peanut butter on my Hevi-Hevian brain. It may seem amusing to you, but the results were very painful to live through.

I hope, hope, hope that it works out for you to visit soon. Until then . . . *Fremmix Bleeblom!*
Your pal,
Pleskit

CHAPTER 2

[TIM]
LUNCH SWAP

I stared at my lunch. A peanut butter sandwich.

Again.

I like peanut butter, but this was getting ridiculous.

"Hey, Pleskit," I said. "What do you have today?"

"*Squambul.* Again! I like *squambul,* but this is getting ridiculous."

I thought for a moment. I had already had one bad experience with alien food. On the other hand, I *was* interested in all things alien. And I was truly, deeply tired of peanut butter.

"Wanna swap?" I asked, holding out my sandwich.

Pleskit looked at it, and a fruity smell drifted from

his *sphen-gnut-ksher.* "Sounds like a good idea to me!" He glanced over at his bodyguard, Robert McNally.

McNally was leaning against the wall about ten feet away. With me being white, Pleskit being purple, and McNally being black, the three of us made a first-rate multicultural group.

McNally was looking in our direction. As usual, he was in supercool mode. Given his dark sunglasses, I couldn't tell if he approved of the lunch swap or not.

Pleskit passed me the *squambul* pod.

I handed my sandwich to Pleskit.

My purple friend sniffed at the bread-and-peanut-butter combination. "The aroma is strange, yet enticing," he said after a moment.

"I can't say the same for this." I coughed, setting the *squambul* on the table.

"You haven't opened it yet. You have to squash it to get the full effect."

"I'm not sure I want the full effect," I said, remembering the hilarious photograph of our enemy Jordan Lynch the first time he had smelled *squambul.* The photo had showed up in *The National News* a week ago. "Maybe we should swap back."

Lunch Swap Disaster

Pleskit's eyes widened, and a smell like burning hair burst from his *sphen-gnut-ksher.* "Please say that you are joking!"

"Hey," I said, "settle down! It's only lunch. Come on, let's swap back."

Very slowly, Pleskit put down the peanut butter sandwich. Placing both hands flat on the table, one on either side of the sandwich, he looked straight into my eyes. "I am asking one more time," he said, his voice deadly serious and tinged with something that sounded like anger. "Tim, are you joking, or do you really mean it?"

I blinked. "Uh . . . I guess I was joking." I reached forward and retrieved the *squambul* pod, astonished by my friend's behavior.

Pleskit let out a heavy breath. His face relaxed into its usual cheerful look. "That's a relief," he said. Then he took a big bite of the sandwich. "Oh my, this is good!" he cried excitedly. "Very good!"

I looked down at the *squambul* pod and wished I had my sandwich back. *Oh well,* I told myself. *If I'm going to be an interstellar explorer, I'm going to have to get used to new and weird stuff. Might as well start with this.*

I squashed the pod between my palms the way I had seen Pleskit do. The sharp odor attacked my nose and made my eyes water.

"Lick it fast, while it's still fresh," said Pleskit. "That's when it's best."

I looked at my palm and shivered. Then I took a deep breath and began to lick the green-and-purple mess.

"Hey," I said, "this isn't bad! Tastes kind of like chicken."

Lunch Swap Disaster

***

Later that afternoon, when we were outside for recess, I said to Pleskit, "So what was that thing at lunch all about?"

"You mean my distress at your violation of the basic social code?" he asked.

"I suppose so. I never saw anyone get so bent out of shape about someone wanting to do a trade back."

"Bent out of shape?" asked Pleskit. He reached up to make sure his *sphen-gnut-ksher* was not disfigured.

"Upset," I clarified, ducking as a soccer ball went flying past my head. "You were really upset. Why?"

Pleskit replied with a question of his own. "What is the Fatherly One's mission all about, Tim?"

I blinked, then said uncertainly, "Uh . . . to establish diplomatic relations, connect Earth to the galaxy, and bring us the benefits of your advanced technology?"

"And why, exactly, would we want to do that?"

"Because you are a wise and benevolent and superior species?"

"So benevolent that we crossed trillions of miles of space just to do you a favor?" His face showed amazement. "Do you really think we came all this way simply because we are *nice*?"

"Uh . . . yes?"

"Uh . . . no."

"Then why did you come?"

"I've told you before, this is a trading mission. It is trade that binds the worlds in friendly alliance. The Fatherly One hopes to find something of value on Earth—something that will let your planet become a trading partner with us."

"You came here to do *business*?" I asked in astonishment.

"Of course! Our whole culture is based on trade. And we are taught from the time we leave the egg that a deal is a deal. We do not make a trade and then expect to be able to trade back instantly if we do not like it. Everything would fall apart if we lived like that. That is why I was so shocked when you wanted to go back on our trade in the cafeteria. It was a warning sign of bad cultural habits."

"Okay, I'm starting to get it," I said. "But what about—"

"Wait!" said Pleskit urgently. *"Look!"*

Lunch Swap Disaster

I turned around. Linnsy Vanderhof, my upstairs neighbor, was walking toward us. I shrugged. "What's the big deal? We see Linnsy every day."

"Are you so blind to beauty?" cried Pleskit. "Is your soul so dead to poetry on the hoof?"

I turned back and stared at Pleskit. "Are you okay?"

"No! I am not okay. I have been pierced by Gorduck's arrow!"

"What?"

"It has gone directly into my *smorgle*!"

"What?" I said again.

He turned to me with a desperate look in his eyes. *"Tim, I am in love!"*

CHAPTER 3

[PLESKIT]
GA-GA-GOOPY!

The *smorgle* is the internal organ of friend-ship and love for a Hevi-Hevian. It is located some-where between the stomach and the heart. It is hard to describe what was happening to mine as Linnsy drew closer. I can only say that I felt a surge of warmth and tenderness.

"Tim," I cried, grasping my friend's arm. "Fountains of joy are rising within me!"

Linnsy stopped and looked at me oddly. "You okay, Pleskit?" she asked.

"Do not be alarmed, my little *squiboodlian*," I crooned. "The music of the spheres is playing just for us." I dropped to my knees. "I do not know the source of this blessed event, but your beauty and the purity of your soul have filled me with a radiant delight hitherto unknown!"

"Pleskit, what's going on?" asked Tim.

"I feel . . . I feel . . . such . . ."

That was when I passed out.

"Pleskit!" said McNally urgently. "Pleskit, are you all right?"

I blinked and discovered I was being held upright by my bodyguard.

"Let me go!" I cried, squirming to escape his grip. "I must speak to my beloved!"

This time McNally actually shouted. "Pleskit! What in heaven's name is wrong with you?"

I blinked and shook my head. I blinked again, then said, "Why are you holding me, McNally?"

"Because you started talking like you'd been taken over by some crazy poet, and then you passed out. I've called for the limo. We're heading back to the embassy. Pronto."

I closed my eyes and took a deep breath. "Could someone please tell me what has been going on?"

"That's what I want to know," said Tim. "We were talking about your weird trade rules when all of a sudden you looked at Linnsy and went all ga-ga-goopy. Next thing I knew, you were spouting ucky loveness at her."

"Yeah," said Linnsy, who had come cautiously back to join us. "What in heck was *that* all about?"

I turned to look at her, and my eyes grew wide.

"About?" I cried. "It was about a feeling so pure and perfect that it shattered my world and nearly burst my *smorgle*. I cannot believe I am lucky enough to stand within a few feet of such beauty!"

"Okay, Pleskit, cut the comedy," she said. "You're not that good at it."

"Let me prove the purity of my feelings!" I cried. I started toward her. As I did, McNally grabbed me and lifted me off the ground again.

"What is going on with you?" he demanded.

"I must tell the most divine creature in the land of my pure and stainless love for her!" I cried, pointing toward Linnsy. I continued to move my feet as if they were still touching the earth.

Other kids had noticed the uproar and were turning in our direction. Most were laughing.

Ms. Weintraub came racing over. "What's going on here?" she cried.

"That's what I want to know," growled McNally.

"Pleskit's lost his mind," said Tim. Getting scientific, he added, "Maybe it's an effect of the atmosphere, or hormones in the water acting on his alien body, or something like that."

With no warning, I felt a change come over me. I stopped squirming and said calmly, "McNally, please put me down."

"Nope," said my bodyguard. "At least, not without a harness."

"Perhaps you could put Pleskit down and just hold his arm, Mr. McNally," said Ms. Weintraub gently.

"Yeah, I suppose I could do that." My bodyguard set me down, but kept a tight grip on my arm. "Don't try anything," he warned.

I glanced around. "I am confused. Also, I do not feel very well. I believe you are right. We should return to the embassy."

"Definitely," said Ms. Weintraub. "You're excused for the rest of the day, Pleskit."

I turned to Linnsy. "If I have caused you distress, I am most sincerely apologetic. I do not know what came over me."

Jordan Lynch, who had joined the crowd surrounding us, said, "You oughta be, you creeper."

"Can it, Jordan!" snapped Ms. Weintraub.

Lunch Swap Disaster

Jordan rolled his eyes. So did Brad Kent, his official tagalong.

Brad always did whatever Jordan did.

Still holding me tightly by the arm, McNally led me off the playground.

"So what was that all about?" asked McNally when we were in the armored limousine that carries us back and forth from the embassy. "Was this step one of another wacko scheme you and Tim have cooked up?"

"No!" I cried earnestly. "I swear by the shards of my egg—and that is an oath that is *meetumlich*, as you can ask the Fatherly One—I am utterly mystified and embarrassed by my own bizarre behavior."

I saw Ralph, the driver, glance at me in his rearview mirror. But he didn't say anything. He never does.

I put my hand on McNally's arm. "Do you think the Fatherly One will be disturbed?"

"Depends. Do guys on your planet usually have complete personality transplants and start swooning over girls?"

"Never!"

"Then he's probably going to be disturbed." He

paused, then added, "Actually, it's the Butt that I'm really worried about."

I groaned. The dreaded Ms. Buttsman! I had nearly forgotten that we would have to face her as well!

CHAPTER 4

[TIM]
LINNSY'S MOM

Linnsy and I walked home together that afternoon, something we had not done much during the last two years, despite the fact that we live in the same apartment building. We had started to pick up the habit again since Pleskit's arrival—mostly because there was so often something disturbing or confusing we needed to discuss.

"Okay," said Linnsy. "If Pleskit going wack-a-doo on the playground today wasn't part of one of your goofy schemes—which I am still not convinced of!—then what *was* it all about?"

"I don't have the slightest idea!"

Linnsy frowned. "You do realize this means big trouble, right?"

"Why? He didn't actually do anything that bad."

Linnsy rolled her eyes. "No. But it was plenty weird. And . . . and this is the important part . . . he doesn't seem to have any idea *why* he did it. Which means it might happen again."

"I'd been thinking about that possibility. I was hoping I was wrong."

"Well, you were right for a change. The question is, what can we do about it?"

For that, I had no answer.

We stopped on the bridge to stare at the embassy. It's located above the central hill in Thorncraft Park, where it dangles from a tall, silvery hook. It looks something like a flying saucer attached to the top part of a coat hanger, except about a thousand times bigger.

"What do you suppose it's like to live in there?" Linnsy asked.

"Only the coolest thing in the universe," I replied. I loved visiting the embassy, with all its weird, otherworldly furnishings.

Lunch Swap Disaster

"I bet it's lonely," said Linnsy. "I bet Pleskit thinks about home a lot."

I snorted. "That's so girl!"

"And you're so dork," replied Linnsy. Then she gave me a little punchie-wunchie, which was what she called it when she socked me on the biceps to try to get me to straighten up. "Come on, let's go see if my mother baked today."

"Why should this day be different from any other day?" I asked, torn between annoyance at the punchie-wunchie and delight at being asked up to Linnsy's place. I could not remember a time I had gone up after school when Mrs. Vanderhof *hadn't* had something just coming out of the oven. Only, I hadn't gone up there very often in the last year or so, after Linnsy and I had drifted into different social groups.

Well, Linnsy had drifted into a social group; I had just drifted, until Pleskit arrived and I finally found someone as weird as myself to hang out with.

"How nice to see you, Mr. Timothy," said Mrs. Vanderhof when we came through the door. ("Mr. Timothy" had been her nickname for me from before I was even in kindergarten.) "You're just in time for some butterscotch brownies."

"Ah," I said, sitting down at the kitchen table. "Just what I was hoping for!" I picked up one of the brownies and took an enormous bite. It was as rich and delicious as I remembered.

"So, how was your day?" asked Mrs. Vanderhof, pulling out a chair to join us.

Linnsy glanced at me uncertainly. I paused, chewed thoughtfully, then gave a nod that indicated I thought she should spill the whole story.

"Well," she said slowly, "it was sort of weird."

Then she told what had happened with Pleskit on the playground.

"Goodness," cried Mrs. Vanderhof, putting her hand to her chest. "It sounds like the last time *I* went crazy."

I choked on my brownie.

CHAPTER 5

[PLESKIT]
WAITING FOR WHOMPIS

Ms. Buttsman is the protocol officer that our host country's government assigned to the embassy to help us navigate the strange ways and customs of Earth. She is very . . . fussy.

"The Butt is definitely not going to like this one," said McNally. "I've got a feeling she keeps a copy of *Politics and Protocol* under her pillow. And believe me, Pleskit, this afternoon's display was anything but politically correct."

I looked at McNally in alarm. "'Politically correct'? Is there going to be a vote about what I did? That is a very disturbing thought. Who will do the voting? The class? The PTA? Or maybe—"

McNally laughed. "'Politically correct' is a way of referring to things you're not supposed to say or do for fear of offending someone, somewhere, somehow. It's a good idea that goes bad when it gets out of control."

"I know how *that* feels," I said ruefully.

At the base of the hill where the embassy is mounted, we have a closely guarded tunnel. This allows us to bypass the crowds that gather every day to gaze at the home of the first aliens to make open contact with Earth.

When McNally and I stepped out of the elevator that carried us from the limousine's underground parking space to the embassy foyer, we found Ms. Buttsman waiting for us. Her face was grim, her arms were crossed, and she was tapping her right foot.

"I've been expecting you," she said coldly. "Principal Grand called a few minutes ago to fill me in on today's events. I'm sure your Fatherly One will have a great deal to say to you about this matter later on, Pleskit."

Lunch Swap Disaster

"How much later?" I asked nervously.

"That depends. Right now we are gathering to greet the ambassador's new assistant. He is due to arrive at any moment."

"Beezle Whompis is actually coming?" I cried. "I had begun to think he would never get here!"

"We received word just a little while ago." She sniffed and added, "Really, I don't think your communication systems are quite as spectacular as you would like us to believe."

I wondered if saying that was politically correct or not.

"Anyway, your Fatherly One was fussing about getting you home from school to be part of the welcome, so it's good that you are here. I haven't yet told him the reason *why* you happened to come home right now. Time enough for that later." She drew in a deep breath and shook her head. "Really, Pleskit, I *am* surprised at you—though I guess I shouldn't be."

"That's all right, Ms. Buttsman," said McNally. "I'm continually surprised at you as well, even though I really ought to be over it by this time."

Ms. Buttsman shot him a sharp look and said, "Walk this way."

I could hardly keep from laughing out loud when McNally followed the woman, doing a perfect imitation of her walk.

The embassy staff had gathered around the shift-stone table in the main meeting room. Shhh-foop, the queen of the kitchen, was singing to herself and waving her orange tentacles in time to her song. Barvgis, round as a beach ball and shining with slime, sat at the end of the table, munching a gnaw stick, which he did whenever he had to go too long without actually eating. The Fatherly One, standing in his usual place, nodded when he saw McNally and me enter. Even the brain of the Grandfatherly One had been put in its transport device and brought into the room.

"When will Beezle Whompis's ship arrive?" I asked, once I had taken my place beside the Fatherly One.

"He's not coming by ship," said Barvgis.

"Then how is he getting here?"

"Electronic transfer," said the Fatherly One, pointing to a metallic device suspended from the ceiling. Dozens of curving purple and blue pipes wound and twisted and looped around one another, finally merging into a trio of tubes that bulged into perfect spheres. Each sphere had a crown-like nozzle at the end. All three nozzles were aimed at the same spot in the center of the table.

Suddenly the device began to glow. Shimmering sparks surged through the tubes, then gathered in the globes, where they swirled frantically around one another.

"Ah, good," said the Fatherly One. "It has begun."

A low hum filled the room. The glow of the pipes grew more intense. The "crowns" pulsed with light. Suddenly the hum changed to a crackling sound. The air seemed charged with power.

"Oh my, my, my, my, my," sang Shhh-foop, pressing three tentacles to her face.

ZZZZZAAAAAAP!

Streams of light flowed from the crowns, merging in the center of the table. A hazy cloud began to develop. Soon it was filled with dancing points of light. It swirled around itself, the points of light moving faster and faster.

A tall, lean form began to take shape. Next came a hissing, sizzling sound from the transfer device, followed by a final burst of energy.

The device went silent and dark.

"E.T. phone home," whispered McNally in awe.

The haze continued to swirl, the form in the center of it slowly becoming more clear and specific until, with a sudden sucking sound, the mist and the light collapsed inward.

Beezle Whompis had arrived.

CHAPTER 6

[TIM]
CRAZY TALK

Linnsy looked at her mother angrily. "Mom!" she said between clenched teeth.

"Oh, for heaven's sake, Linnsy," said Mrs. Vanderhof. "There is no reason for Tim not to know about what happened."

"Yes, there is," said Linnsy.

Mrs. Vanderhof shook her head slightly and said, "I refuse to take part in my own repression." Her voice was calm, but very serious. "If more people would be open about this kind of thing, there wouldn't be so much shame and fear attached to it—which would mean that more people would get help when they needed it."

Lunch Swap Disaster

Linnsy sighed, rolled her eyes, and crossed her arms over her chest. "I suppose you're going to talk about this whether I want you to or not."

"It makes a good test, dear," said Mrs. Vanderhof cheerfully. "You'll find that people who can't handle it aren't worth hanging around with." She turned to me. "Do you remember a night about two years ago when your mom got a sudden call to come up here?"

"Not really," I said. Then I blinked. "Oh, wait—was that the time you went away for a couple of weeks? Whoa! Don't tell me you were in the loony bin all that time!"

"See what I mean?" cried Linnsy.

My eyes widened in horror as I realized what I had just blurted out. "Ack! I'm sorry! I didn't mean to say that! It just . . . I mean . . . Omigosh, I am *so* sorry."

I glanced down at the floor, vaguely hoping a giant hole would open and swallow me into another dimension.

Mrs. Vanderhof sighed and shook her head wearily. "I'd be angrier if I weren't so used to it."

"So why can't you just keep quiet about it?" asked Linnsy savagely.

"I can handle it," I said. "Really, I can. I was just startled. Honest."

"Besides, when you get right down to it, I *was* loony at the time," said Mrs. Vanderhof. "Someone listening to me might have found my ramblings pretty hilarious, or pretty scary. Or both, I suppose. For me, it was exciting and scary all at once. I felt I knew things that no one else knew, understood the world in a way that no one else ever had."

"She left messages all over the house, explaining the secret meaning of things," said Linnsy.

"If I remember correctly, I told you the toaster held the answer to world peace," said Mrs. Vanderhof with a laugh. "Yet for all that I felt I had secret knowledge, at the same time I was terrified. I knew I was out of control, but I didn't know what to do about it." She turned and looked out the window for a moment. "I imagine it was pretty scary for those around me as well."

"You're not kidding," said Linnsy. She turned to me. "When I got home from school that day, Mom was sitting in the middle of the living room floor. She had her suitcase next to her, her camera around her neck, and a flashlight in her hand. When I asked what was going on, she said she was waiting for the aliens to come and take her back where she came from."

Lunch Swap Disaster

"But that was two years before the aliens had even made contact," I said. Then I blinked. "Oh. I see."

Mrs. Vanderhof smiled ruefully. "I had found a card inviting Linnsy to a birthday party with an alien theme. In my condition, I took it to mean some aliens were inviting me to be their queen."

Linnsy rolled her eyes. "When I walked in, she was singing the theme song from *Tarbox Moon Warriors*. She told me she had made a week's worth of cookies, but after that I would be on my own because she had to return to her true home in the stars."

"Actually, dear, I think I told you that you could come along."

Linnsy laughed. "Yeah, but only if I ate a dozen of your secret rocket cookies first." She turned to me. "I was terrified. Dad was out of town on a business trip. And Mom seemed so convinced of what she was saying that I almost believed her—though I got over that when she started having a conversation with my teddy bear."

"I thought he was Captain Norf-Norf," explained Mrs. Vanderhof. "I think that was when Linnsy called your mom and asked for help."

"But you seem so . . ." I searched for a word. "So *normal*," I finally said, somewhat lamely.

"I am normal! At least, I am when my blood chemistry is working properly. When my chemistry is off, I can leave reality so far behind it looks as if I'll never see it again. But as soon as they get my meds properly adjusted, I start coming back in for a landing."

"So, are all crazy people like that?" I closed my eyes in embarrassment. "Sorry. But you know what I mean."

Mrs. Vanderhof shook her head. "Mental illness comes in a lot of different flavors, Tim. Some of the people in what you called 'the loony bin' are in for the long haul—or at least, they are until some breakthrough in treatment occurs. Others are folk who have had their cup of sorrow filled way beyond the brim; they've made a temporary retreat from sanity because it's more than they can cope with. And some are like me, people with a short-term problem that can be fixed fairly simply by getting their chemistry straightened out. The thing is, despite all we've learned, most of the world still reacts to mental problems as if there is some deep shame about them. But what I deal with is no more shameful than diabetes or a heart problem."

"In your opinion," said Linnsy.

"In reality," her mother replied firmly. "The problem is, people haven't had time to get used to that idea. A hundred years ago, odds are good I would have spent my life in an institution—just for lack of the right medicine!"

A new question, a somewhat frightening one, occurred to me. Trying not to sound too nervous, I asked, "This condition, isn't, uh . . . catching, is it?"

Mrs. Vanderhof laughed. "You can't catch it just by being near me, if that's what you're worried about. Can't catch it at all, actually. It's something you're born with, though it sometimes takes a long time to show up."

"Okay, I've got the picture. But what does this all have to do with Pleskit?"

Mrs. Vanderhof shrugged and reached for a brownie. "I'm not sure. It's just that, from your description, he moved in and out of this strange condition so fast that it sounded like a speeded-up version of what I sometimes go through." She glanced at me and laughed. "Oh, stop looking so worried! I went seven years between my first 'episode' and the one

I told you about. I'm not going to wack out on you in the next thirty seconds. The good news is, we're understanding more about mental illness all the time. I know your dream is to explore the vast reaches of outer space. But the truth is, there's a whole universe inside our heads that we've barely begun to discover." She tapped me on the forehead. "Between your ears lies a vast, uncharted wilderness."

"That's definitely true for Tim," Linnsy said with a laugh. "Who knows what weirdness lurks between *those* ears?"

My search for a withering response was interrupted by the phone.

"It's for you, Mr. Timothy," Mrs. Vanderhof said a moment later.

I took the receiver.

It was my mother. "Tim, I think you'd better get down here," she said. "Pronto!"

CHAPTER 7

[PLESKIT]
ALIEN ARRIVAL

We burst into applause—each of us showing approval in the way specific to his, her, or its planet. The Fatherly One belched heartily. Barvgis slapped his hands against his own shoulders, shouting, *"Pooong! Pooong! Poong!"* Shhh-foop swirled her tentacles, causing them to emit a hissing sound. I burped. But at the same time I felt a small twist of fear, which caused me to feel angry with myself. I had already lived on three previous worlds (four, if you count Geembol Seven, which I prefer not to). I knew enough not to fear someone merely because of appearance.

Even so, keeping fear at bay is not always easy. So I

studied the newcomer, because I know that for beings of goodwill, knowledge usually displaces fear.

Beezle Whompis was at least seven feet tall and completely bald. His enormous, deep-set eyes were the most prominent feature of his thin, almost cadaverous, face. His skin, which looked like dry, yellowed *flegstik*, was stretched tightly over sunken cheeks. Three rounded nostrils in the otherwise flat center of his face gave the tiniest hint of a nose. An elegant robe hung from his bony shoulders, reaching nearly to his feet.

He gazed at our little group, then shook himself from head to foot, as if he had just experienced a chill.

"Well, *that* was an interesting trip," he said, seeming to speak mostly to himself. Turning to the Fatherly One, he bowed slightly and added, "Beezle Whompis, reporting for service."

"Welcome, Beezle Whompis," said the Fatherly One. "We have been eagerly awaiting your arrival."

"I am pleased to be here," said Beezle Whompis, inclining his head slightly. "My apologies for the delay. Things at my last assignment became unexpectedly complicated. Just one problem after another, if you know what I mean." He waved his skeletal fingers in front of his face in a complicated gesture.

"Well, if that's what you're used to, you're going to feel right at home here," muttered McNally.

Ms. Buttsman shot him an icy glare.

"I have never seen one of those transfers done before," said Barvgis. "It was very impressive."

Beezle Whompis bowed his head in acknowledgment. Then he shimmered and disappeared. A moment later he was standing on the floor next to Ms. Buttsman. She uttered a tiny shriek, then clapped her hand to her mouth and began to blush.

"Forgive me, Ms. Buttsman," said the Fatherly One. "I should have given you more information regarding our new staff member. Beezle Whompis is a . . ." He paused, as if searching for a word.

"Allow me," said Beezle Whompis. Turning to Ms. Buttsman, he said, "I am a—"

The last "word" of his sentence was a harsh, grinding sound, like static on a radio. He smiled, or made something like a smile, since though his mouth curved up, it still drooped at the corners. "Think of me as a discorporate entity. My people do not have bodies—at least, not as you use the term. I take on this form merely as a matter of . . . politeness. I have found it is easier for the flesh-bound to relate to me if they can see me like this."

"How . . . interesting," said Ms. Buttsman, edging away from him.

"I would shake your hand in standard Earth greeting," continued Beezle Whompis, "but doing so would cause all your hair to stand on end, which my studies have indicated you would not appreciate."

"Sounds like fun to me," said McNally as Ms. Buttsman patted her hair nervously.

"I am most eager to experience all of you," said Beezle Whompis, turning to face the others at the table. "But first, Ambassador, I beg a moment in private. I must deliver an urgent message."

I watched in dismay as the Fatherly One and Beezle Whompis left the meeting room to head for the Fatherly One's private office.

"What do you suppose the message is?" I asked once the door had closed behind them.

Ms. Buttsman—who seemed to be recovering from her shock at meeting Beezle Whompis—said primly, "I'm sure it's adult business and no concern of yours, Pleskit."

Lunch Swap Disaster

"You are a source of unending joy, Ms. Buttsman," said McNally.

Ms. Buttsman gave him a tight smile. "Don't forget that when Meenom is done with Beezle Whompis, he will want to speak to Pleskit about what happened at school today. I expect he will want to discuss it with you, too, Mr. McNally." She looked around the room. "Well! That's settled, I think. Mr. Whompis has made it here safely, so why don't we all just get back to our jobs?"

And with that she left the room.

"Someone must be feeding that lady bad food," sang Shhh-foop, whirling several of her tentacles. She turned to Pleskit. "Singing of food—would you like a snackie-doodle, my little Pleskit-pie?"

"Sounds like a good idea," I said glumly.

"I don't suppose you have anything for me?" asked Barvgis hopefully.

"Of course," sang Shhh-foop. "Always lots to eat for the pleasingly plump. And perhaps a cup of coffee for the handsome guarder of Pleskit's body?"

"Uh, sure," said McNally nervously. He liked Shhh-foop, but her attempts at coffee had all been hideous failures.

Bruce Coville

Our little group had no sooner gathered in the kitchen than a red light flashed above the door. We heard a slight hissing sound. Then a sharp smell drifted through the room.

Barvgis sighed. "I guess my snack will have to wait, Shhh-foop. I have been summoned."

"Come back soon!" sang Shhh-foop, waving her tentacles in farewell. Then she slapped two of them against the counter to summon the coffeepot.

Barvgis left the room, mournfully patting his very round midsection as he went. Shhh-foop slid across the floor with a cup of coffee. She placed it delicately in front of McNally, then slid back a few feet and watched him anxiously, several of her tentacles twitching just a bit.

McNally sniffed it, then raised it to his lips and took a cautious sip. His eyes widened, and he looked slightly terrified. "Not quite, Shhh-foop," he said hoarsely. Staring at the steaming coffee as if it might bite him, he returned the cup to the table.

"Woe, woe is she who cannot coax true joy from the bean of caffeine for Just McNally," crooned Shhh-foop sadly as she slid back to the counter. She returned a moment later with a tray of squeaking purple cubes, which she placed in front of me. *"Pak-skwardles,"* she sang proudly.

"Great!" I cried, scooping one into my mouth. I turned to my bodyguard. "Want some, McNally? They're delicious."

"Uh—I think I'll go to my room now," said McNally. "I'll catch you later, Pleskit. Good luck with your Fatherly One."

"Oy," I said, using a word I had learned from my Grandfatherly One's brain.

It did not take long for the summons to come. When it did, I popped a last *pak-skwardle* into my mouth for comfort, then trudged out of the kitchen. My pet Veeblax joined me in the corridor. It took on a four-legged shape, then walked beside me, cooing sympathetically.

To reach the Fatherly One's office, I first had to pass through an outer office, where his assistant held guard. When I reached this room, I was startled to see Beezle Whompis already sitting in the chair that had been occupied by Mikta-makta-mookta, until her villainous plans to sabotage the mission had been revealed.

The new assistant nodded as I came in. "Your Fatherly One said to send you in the moment you got here," he said. Then he vanished—only to pop up directly next to me, which caused me to jump in surprise.

"Sorry," said Beezle Whompis. "I should remember it takes you physical beings a while to get used to that. Listen, I've gone over the messages from school today, and the situation is not pleasant. I thought I should warn you that your parental unit is most distressed."

He vanished again, only to reappear in the chair where he had been sitting a moment earlier.

I blinked and headed into the office, the Veeblax at my heels.

The Fatherly One's command pod was floating halfway between floor and ceiling.

"You wished to see me, Parental Unit?" I asked, looking up and feeling small.

"I have had a disturbing report from the school, my childling." He paused, then added significantly, "Another one."

Lunch Swap Disaster

I hung my head. "I have no excuse, parent/mentor.
An unbearable urge came over me most unexpectedly.
At first I did not even realize what was happening."

The Fatherly One burped a command, and the pod drifted gently to the floor. He stepped out, put his hands on my shoulders, and said, "I need you to exercise caution and control right now. Especially control. Obviously it will take time for us to learn all the little ways in which things in this planet's environment may affect us. But you cannot use that as an excuse! You must contain your impulses." He paused, then continued, "This is a perilous moment for our mission."

The fear I felt now had nothing to do with the Fatherly One's anger. "I do not understand," I said quietly.

"I will explain," said the Fatherly One. His face was heavy with concern.

CHAPTER 8

[TIM]
COMMUNICATION

When I got down to our apartment, I found a large purple package sitting in the center of the living room floor.

"It's from the embassy," said Mom. "Ralph the driver dropped it off about five minutes ago. He said Pleskit wants you to open it as soon as possible. I figured you'd want to know right away. He also left a note," she added, passing me a small purple envelope.

"This is too cool!" I cried. "I wonder what it is." I stuffed the envelope into my pocket, then grabbed the package and began trying to open it.

Five minutes later, I was snarling with frustration.

The wrapping material, whatever it was, was impossible to cut or tear in any way.

"May I offer a suggestion?" asked my mother.

"What?" I snapped.

"Never mind. If you can't speak civilly, I'll keep my stupid adult thoughts to myself."

I sighed. "Sorry. What's your suggestion?"

"Why not check what's in the envelope?"

Feeling foolish, I pulled the envelope from my pocket. Unlike the package, it opened easily.

Tim:

Greetings and good wishes!

I have finally arranged for us to have a more effective method of communication than your primitive telephone system provides. At last I will be able to see you and smell you when we talk, rather than simply hearing you! (You will be able to smell me as well. However, I know this is not a particularly effective means of communication for Earthlings, so you can switch off the odor emitter if it bothers you.)

Batteries are not included, mostly because they are embargoed technology. I'm not sure why I can send you the communicator and not the batteries, unless the Trading Federation has determined that your scientists might be able to figure out how to make the batteries, while the communicator would be beyond them. Anyway, we had to come up with another power source, which is part of why this has taken so long. Barvgis finally reconfigured the device so you can plug it into a standard Earth socket. It disturbed me to do so, but he said it was the best solution, inelegant though it appears.

To open the package, just run your fingertip along the edges of the box. It has been cued to your personal chemistry, which we have on record from your trips to the embassy.

Please contact me as soon as you have the unit up and running. I had a very disturbing conversation with the Fatherly One this afternoon, and I want to discuss it with you.

Looking forward to seeing/hearing/smell-
ing you.

Fremmix Bleeblom!
Your pal,
Pleskit

I looked at my fingertip, not certain I liked the idea
that the aliens had so much information on file about
me. But I was too curious to spend much time worry-
ing about that, so I ran my fingertip along the edges of
the box. Instantly the sides, top, and bottom rolled into
small tubes. Without a sound, the tubes slid one into
another. A second later, all that remained of the box
was something that looked like a long, purple straw.

"I wonder how this thing works," said Mom, picking
up the slender tube. "I'd love to have a bunch of these
at Christmastime. I'd save hours of wrapping!"

I was too intrigued by the contents of the box to
answer. The base of the object was circular, about
an inch thick and maybe eight or nine inches across.
Mounted on this base was something that would have
looked like a computer monitor, if monitors were circular

and no thicker than a penny. On the base was a single purple button, shaped like an egg.

"Gotta go check this out," I said, picking up the machine. I carried it to my room, where it took me a few minutes to clear a spot among the comic books, action figures, and dirty laundry to set the thing, then plugged it in.

I reached out and touched the button on the base.

The circular screen began to glow. A pair of small boxes folded out from the base. Then two metallic tentacles stretched up from the boxes. They reminded me of the extensions that came from the brain vat of Pleskit's Grandfatherly One.

"Do you wish to make contact?" asked a pleasant voice.

"Yes!" I shouted, so excited, I could barely stay in my chair.

"Such volume is not necessary," said the voice, sounding as if it were wincing. "With whom do you wish to be connected?"

"Pleskit."

"Noted and logged. I will let you know when contact is—"

The voice was cut off, and Pleskit's face appeared on the screen. "Tim!" he said happily. "You got it working!"

"This is so cool!" I said. "Can you see me?"

Pleskit blinked, as if surprised by the question. "Of course. That was the point. I can smell you too, which makes the communication much more complete — though the odor from your underwear pile sends more information than I really want to know." He leaned closer to the screen. "Are you alone?"

"Yeah, I'm in my room. Mom tries to avoid coming in here, on account of the mess makes her upset."

"Good. I need to talk to you."

Lunch Swap Disaster

"What's up? Wait! Did you get in trouble about what happened at school today?"

"The Fatherly One was surprisingly understanding, though he did get cranky about the fact that I brought the Veeblax into his office with me. But listen, Tim. My strange behavior today is not the only thing going on. There are other problems here—problems that are very disturbing for the future of your planet."

CHAPTER 9

[PLESKIT]

TIM HAS A BRAINSTORM

Tim frowned. "That doesn't sound so good."

"It's not. The Fatherly One's new assistant arrived today—"

"Beezle Whompis finally got here?" interrupted Tim. "I was beginning to think he was never coming. Is he cool?"

"Please, do not start again with 'cool,'" I said. I still had not been able to totally grasp the idea. "Let's just say he is . . . unusual. The important thing right now is that he brought a message from the Interplanetary Trading Federation." I took a deep breath. "Things do not look good for the mission."

Lunch Swap Disaster

Tim's eyes grew wide. "Why not?"

"The beings who are monitoring us feel that the Fatherly One is not progressing rapidly enough toward his goals."

"Geez, Pleskit, you've only been here a few weeks. What do they want?"

"It's not so much what he hasn't done as it is how many things have gone wrong. We have had a remarkable number of . . . incidents, given the brief time we have been here."

"It's not like Mikta-makta-mookta was your fault!" said Tim indignantly. "She was *assigned* to you guys by the Trading Federation."

"That is true," I agreed. "However, even in an advanced civilization, people like to shift blame whenever they can. And the Fatherly One makes an easy target because of what happened on Geembol Seven."

"Which I still want to know more about," said Tim.

My *sphen-gnut-ksher* emitted a gust of odor, which the communicator sent straight through to Tim. He flinched. "Man, Pleskit," he said, waving his hand in front of his face. "If you don't want to talk about it, just say so. You don't have to stink up my whole room!"

"Sorry. Involuntary reaction. Tap the top of the device twice if you want to turn off the odor transmitter."

"Whew," Tim said a minute later, still waving his hand in front of his face. "That's better. So, what do the top guys at the Trading Federation want?"

"Well, Beezle Whompis says the best thing we could do right now is show progress in finding something that can be used for interstellar trade." I wanted to emit the smell of deep concern but knew that Tim would not understand, even if he had not turned off the odor transmitter. So instead I put on my most serious expression and said, "If things do not get better soon, the Fatherly One may lose his franchise."

"Just how bad would that be?"

"Very bad for us—even worse for you."

"What does *that* mean?"

"Most beings who have studied the situation—and there aren't that many, because Earth is still considered a very minor planet—think it would be better to simply colonize your planet."

"Colonize it?" asked Tim uneasily.

"Take it over," I said bluntly. "The Fatherly One is considered a real *beezledorf* for the way he wants to deal with you. But he staked the first claim, so his wishes have to be honored—unless the Federation decides he has not exploited the franchise properly."

"And if they do decide that?"

"Then we're out, and someone else—someone much tougher—takes over the planet. We have come hoping to be partners. The next to come would more likely be conquerors."

"Yikes!"

"Precisely. The problem for us is finding something worth trading. Frankly, Earth does not have much to offer. Certainly not your technology, which is far behind ours. You might provide a good workforce, but that would take lots of training."

"What about our natural resources?" asked Tim. "Haven't you guys all, like, plundered your planets and ruined your ecologies and stuff?"

I laughed. "Do you think we are idiots? Earth *is* potentially one of the fairest and richest planets in the galaxy. Unfortunately, it is currently also one of the worst managed. According to the Fatherly One, the first survey team wept in frustration when they saw what you people have done to the place."

"Well, that makes me feel just wonderful," said Tim.

"Don't take it personally. However, it would probably be just as well if your room was never exposed to off-planet scrutiny."

"Ha, very ha."

I smiled. "Oh good. I made a joke! But do not worry. The problem at the moment has much less to do with you than it does with me. Today's events at school only added to the sense that the mission is being mismanaged. Botched. Tim, I do not want to be responsible for costing the Fatherly One yet another planetary assignment!"

"But what happened today wasn't really your fault," said Tim.

"Well, I certainly didn't do it on purpose. But it happened nonetheless."

"Right, so the question is . . ." Tim stopped. His eyes widened. "Hold on! I think I've got it!"

"You think you've got what?" I asked in alarm. "Do you mean it's catching? Are you going to start having inappropriate bursts of emotion too?"

Tim snorted. "As if! I mean, I think I know what set you off today."

Lunch Swap Disaster

"What?"

"Think about it. What did you do today that was different from most days? Think lunch, Pleskit."

"Peanut butter!" I cried. "I ate your peanut butter sandwich!" My *sphen-gnut-ksher* bent sideways in a questioning gesture. "Do you really think that was the source of my bizarre actions?"

"Makes as much sense as anything else. Do you have any way to check it out?"

"Certainly. We can explore the idea the same way we would explore any other hypothesis."

"And how would that be?"

"By conducting an experiment."

CHAPTER 10

[TIM]

EXPERIMENT

"I love experiments!" I cried. Then I wrinkled my brow. "What do you have in mind?"

"It should be obvious. We feed me some peanut butter, then put me in a room with a female of your species and see what happens."

"Excellent idea! I don't want to try this at the embassy. Can you arrange for Linnsy to come down to your apartment? I will see if I can get McNally to bring me over."

"Good. Then you can give me some more instructions for using this communication thingie," I said. "I'm going by the seat of my pants right now."

Lunch Swap Disaster

"There is no need to show it your backside!" cried Pleskit. "I did not think you Earthlings had sufficient control of your farting mechanism to give the device commands that way, so Barvgis reprogrammed it to be more sensitive to spoken language. I am sorry I underestimated your communication skills."

I sighed. "I just meant . . . oh, never mind. I'll call you back as soon as I've talked to Linnsy. If you don't hear from me in ten minutes, you better call me, because it may mean I'm having trouble with the machine. Hmm. Better make it fifteen. Convincing Linnsy may take a while."

"I may have the same problem with McNally," said Pleskit. "He is officially off duty. Therefore, some pleading is likely to be required to get him to bring me over." He made a long, multi-toned belch, smiled, and said, "That means: 'Talk to you/see you/smell you soon.'"

The communicator went dark.

I went to call Linnsy on the regular phone.

Her first response was pretty much what I had expected.

"You want me to *what*?"

"We want you to participate in an experiment that could help determine the future of Earth-alien relationships," I said, trying to sound reassuring. "Controlled conditions. Perfectly safe. Could be crucial to life as we know it."

"Hold on," said Linnsy. "Let me check the weather report. Aha! Just as I thought. 'Cloudy, with a chance of wackos.'"

"Linnsy!"

"Tim!"

Click.

I called her back.

"Hi. It's me."

"Like, big surprise."

"Come on, Linns. There's nothing to worry about. McNally will be here, and Pleskit will be . . . immobilized. We just need to check out my theory."

"You need to check out your brain!"

Click.

I called her back again. Before I could even say her name, she shouted, "Will you stop bothering me?"

"Not until you help us save the world."

"Give me one good reason," said Linnsy.

"Saving the world isn't enough of a reason?" I yelped.

Lunch Swap Disaster

"Give me one good reason why this idiotic idea has anything to do with saving the world."

I hesitated, then said, "Can I trust you?"

"Can *you* trust *me*?" she cried. "I don't think that's the question here, buddy."

I took a deep breath, then went on. "Look, Linnsy, Pleskit's Fatherly One is the good guy in all this. He's trying to be a partner with us Earthlings. If he gets recalled by the Interplanetary Trading Federation, the next trader who gets the Earth franchise may decide we should be a colony instead."

Linnsy went silent for so long that I began to wonder if she had put the phone down and walked away. Finally she whispered, "Tim, are you messing with me on this? Because if you are—"

"Tarbox's Honor, Linnsy," I said, which effectively cut off her question. She knew good and well that while I might like to wiggle around on the edges of reality a bit, when I used the Tarbox oath, I was deadly serious.

She sighed. "I'll be there."

It was early evening. Gathered in the living room of our apartment were me, Pleskit, McNally, and my mother.

Linnsy was waiting in the kitchen.

"Are you sure this is a good idea?" Mom said nervously.

I sighed. "I've told you what's at stake, Mom. Besides, McNally is here to keep Pleskit in line—which he won't even need to do unless my theory is correct."

"I concur with Tim's analysis," said Pleskit. He was sitting in a straight-backed wooden chair. McNally stood behind him.

Mom sighed. "What about you, Mr. McNally?"

The bodyguard shrugged. "I think it's worth a shot."

Mom stepped forward and gingerly placed a peanut butter sandwich on the tray table I had set up by Pleskit's chair.

"Divine aroma," said Pleskit, picking up the sandwich and sniffing it.

Then he took a bite.

We watched him anxiously.

"I think I should probably eat the whole sandwich," he said. "Also, even if this is the source of the problem, it may take a while for it to kick in."

He took another bite of the sandwich, and then another.

Lunch Swap Disaster

I got too impatient to wait for him to finish, and I motioned for Linnsy to come in.

The moment she entered, Pleskit put down the sandwich. He sat back in his chair as if he had been stunned. McNally put his hands on Pleskit's shoulders.

"Let me go, McNally!" cried Pleskit. "Gorduck, the god of love, has pierced my *clinkus* with the flaming arrows of pure bliss. I have seen my future, and she is Linnsy!"

"Pleskit!" snapped McNally. "Get ahold of yourself."

"You'd better go wait in the kitchen, Linnsy," I said quietly.

Eyes wide, Linnsy slipped out of the room. As soon as she was gone, Pleskit slumped down in the chair.

"Hypothesis proven," I said. "Pleskit can*not* handle his peanut butter."

"That's the worst allergic reaction I've seen since Aunt Louise accidentally ate the shrimp salad," said Mom, her voice a little shaky. "I think I need some coffee. Would you like a cup, Mr. McNally?"

"Love some. But I'd better wait till we're sure Pleskit's under control."

Pleskit groaned. "This is the most humiliating

thing I have ever experienced. Please carry my apologies to Linnsy."

"It's okay!" shouted Linnsy from the kitchen. "Just don't get near me for the time being."

"I am a walking social catastrophe," said Pleskit mournfully.

"Nah, you're just another victim of biology," said McNally. "If we keep you away from peanut butter, you should be fine."

That, however, proved to be more easily said than done.

CHAPTER 11

[PLESKIT]
THINGS GET STICKIER

"Pleskit Meenom, report to the office. I repeat: Pleskit Meenom, please report to the office."

"*Zgribnick!*" I muttered, as my *sphen-gnut-ksher* emitted the mid-range odor of distress.

"Geez, Pleskit," said Tim. "That smell reminds me of a piece of baloney I accidentally left under my bed for several months last year."

McNally stood to go with me.

"Looks like your reputation has caught up with you, lover boy," hooted Jordan.

"Pack it in, Jordan!" snapped Ms. Weintraub. "Pleskit has already explained what happened yesterday."

***

Mr. Grand sat behind his desk, looking very serious.

I stood in front of him, feeling very nervous.

McNally leaned against the back wall, showing no expression at all.

"I have heard disturbing rumors about an event that occurred on the playground yesterday," said Mr. Grand, steepling his fingertips in front of his face.

"I can explain everything, sir," I said.

"Please do."

I did. When I was done, Mr. Grand shook his head and said sadly, "Really, Pleskit? I honestly expected better of you."

"But it's true!" I cried.

"Your behavior was bad enough," Mr. Grand said, taking a sour ball out of the jar he always kept on his desk. "But trying to shift the blame in this silly fashion—*peanut butter*, for heaven's sake!—is even worse. Better by far, my young interstellar traveler, to simply accept responsibility for your actions. That is more honorable, more manly. It is the Earthling way."

He bit down on the sour ball. "Now, I want a promise from you that this behavior will not be repeated. I will work very hard to keep word of it from leaking to the press—you know what kind of trouble we have when they get their noses into something like this. But you have to work with me here, Pleskit. You simply can't go around exhibiting such outrageous behavior and expect to have no consequences."

"Am I going to be punished?" I asked uneasily.

"Not this time. But if it should happen again—well, punishment aside, I fear we could end up in court! The world does not take such behavior lightly these days. Now, no more of this nonsense about peanut butter. Simply control yourself, and everything will be fine. If you feel an urge to spout poetry to one of the girls, take a deep breath, count to ten, and just say no. You can go now."

That afternoon, the girls on the playground giggled and pointed when I walked by. So I was happy, if a bit surprised, when Linnsy came to stand with me.

"Just figured that me standing with you might calm things down a bit," she said.

To my delight, it seemed to work. After a few minutes Misty Longacres and Rafaella Martinez wandered over to talk with me as well.

"Girls have secret ways of communicating," said Tim softly.

"Really?" I asked. "Do they do it with smells?"

"Beats me," said Tim. "Maybe it's just some kind of secret language. I only know that it happens and I don't understand it."

The next day Ms. Weintraub announced that the science fair would take place earlier than usual this year. "You'll need to start thinking about your projects soon," she said. "Here's a list of possibilities."

"Pleskit can do something on peanut butter allergies," said Jordan with a snicker.

"Allergies are very serious business," replied Larrabe Hicks, who was definitely the most serious boy in our class.

"So is terminal dorkhood," said Jordan.

"What, exactly, is a science fair?" I asked.

"It's one of the most exciting events of the school year," said Ms. Weintraub. "Each of you will choose a topic to research. You'll do some experimenting, prepare a report, and even more important, figure out ways to demonstrate what you have learned. At the end, all of you bring your projects to the gym, and we all get to see what everyone has done."

"You could die from the thrills," muttered Jordan.

"I am sorry your metabolism is not sufficient to deal with the excitement," I said. "From my point of view, it sounds like fun."

"We'll pick our subjects next week and start serious work the week after that," said Ms. Weintraub.

The next couple of days were quiet. Tim and I talked every night on the new comsystem, mostly discussing ways we could convince our parental units to allow a sleepover. Ms. Weintraub distributed a list of suggestions for science fair projects. Homework was assigned. Tests were taken. Spitballs were thrown.

Then, on Friday afternoon, Brad Kent offered me a cookie.

I was slightly startled by this, as Brad had never been particularly friendly toward me. However, it is a truth of diplomatic relations that the sharing of food is one of the prime ways of building personal connections on almost every planet. So, wary, but not wanting to offend, I accepted Brad's offer.

"Hmmm," I said, sniffing. "A delectable aroma. Slightly familiar, and . . ." I closed my eyes and took a deeper breath. "Ah, yes. *Irresistible!*"

CHAPTER 12

[TIM]
ALIEN ROMEO

Out of the corner of my eye, I noticed Brad handing Pleskit the cookie. I was talking with Linnsy when it happened, and at first it didn't register as anything suspicious. But even as we continued to talk, my brain began asking questions—questions such as:

Why is Jordan's official flunky and chief butt-kisser offering Pleskit a cookie?

Can this possibly be a good thing?

If not, why not?

And then came the key question: *What kind of cookies has Brad Kent brought to school at least once a week every year since first grade?*

The answers came rushing together in a moment of terror. "Pleskit!" I cried. *"Don't eat that cookie!"*

It was too late. Even as I cried out for him to stop and McNally lunged forward to grab it from him, Pleskit had taken a bite.

Another dose of peanut butter had just entered my alien friend's bloodstream.

"What's the matter?" cried Pleskit, his *sphen-gnut-ksher* emitting an odor unlike anything I had ever smelled before.

"Peanut butter!" I cried. "Pleskit, that's a peanut butter cookie!"

Pleskit's eyes widened. The odor from his *sphen-gnut-ksher* changed to the now familiar burning-hair smell that indicated panic. He held the remainder of the cookie away from him, staring at it in horror.

McNally snatched it from Pleskit's hand, sniffed it, took a bite. "That's peanut butter, all right," he said grimly.

"Gosh, Pleskit, I'm sorry," said Brad, and I could tell he was trying to control the smile twitching at the corners of his mouth. "I didn't even think about that."

I glanced to my side. Jordan was leaning against

the building, holding his sides and squeezing his eyes shut as he tried to contain his laughter.

"You okay, Pleskit?" asked McNally.

Pleskit placed his hands on his stomach and closed his eyes. "I think I will be all right, O Guardian of My Well-Being. I took only one bite, and now that we know what to anticipate, I hope/expect I will be able to control my reaction. Even so, perhaps we should go inside for now."

"Good idea," said McNally.

As they left the playground, I stalked over to Jordan and said angrily, "That was a rotten thing to do!"

"What?" cried Jordan, spreading his hands. "What did I do?" His eyes were wide with fake innocence, and he could barely get the words past his ongoing attempts to control his laughter.

"You know what I mean," I snapped. "You *told* Brad to give Pleskit that cookie!"

"Why, Tim, I wouldn't do a thing like that to your little purple pal. Besides, it's not like I control Brad or anything. Anyway, that peanut butter stuff is just an excuse Pleskit was using to get out of trouble. My father says its total baloney."

"It is not!" I said fiercely.

Jordan yawned in my face.

"It's jerks like you who give Earthlings a bad name!" I yelled.

I turned to stalk away. Jordan deftly stuck out one foot, tripped me, and sent me sprawling facedown in the dirt of the playground.

"It's people like you who give clumsiness a bad name," he said mockingly.

"Maybe you should join Dweebs Anonymous," hooted Brad, who had slid over to stand beside Jordan.

Laughing uproariously, the two of them walked away.

CHAPTER 13

[PLESKIT]
ME AND MY BIG MOUTH

When the class came back from recess, I was sprawled on top of my desk, leaning on one arm. "Why, Ms. Weintraub," I said. "You're looking sweeter than a *skibwee* today."

A faint, flowery smell drifted from my *sphen-gnut-ksher.*

Ms. Weintraub blinked in surprise, then said firmly, "Pleskit, take your seat!"

I sighed but did as she asked. I rested my chin on my hands and stared at my teacher longingly—until Misty Longacres walked past, at which point I turned and said, "Misty. Ah, Misty. A name like a poem. Was yours the face that stilled all hearts at Kilgaddurr? Are those the hands that wove the *sheelkirk*'s robe?"

"What's with that alien trash talk?" snapped Misty.

"Don't mind me," I murmured. "It's part of an old poem from Hevi-Hevi."

As I thought about that poem, and the dramatic gesture that its hero, Morcandus, makes in honor of his love, I felt a sudden eruption of joy in my *smorgle*. Suddenly I knew that I, too, had to make a grand gesture. Without a word I leaped from my desk and raced to the main office. I vaguely wondered where McNally was, but since he was not there to stop me, I didn't truly care.

Mr. Grand's secretary was not at her desk. The door to Mr. Grand's office was closed. I was alone. Perfect!

I crossed to the control board for the school's public address system. It should have been easy to use, but the technology was so primitive that it took me a few moments to figure out how to work it. Once I got it, I was surprised at how simple it was. I flipped a switch, then picked up the microphone.

"Attention, students," I said. "This is your alien friend, Pleskit Meenom, and I wish to tell you of the great joy that fills my heart in being a part of this school. Truly, it is a wonderful thing to be here with you, even with Jordan Lynch, who has tried to sabotage my time here. I am too filled with love and gratitude to let his treachery bother me now.

"Now I must speak of the even greater joy that fills me when I consider the honor and delight of being in the class of Ms. Weintraub, who is possibly the most beautiful teacher in the known universe. She walks in clouds of glory, and has the heart of a *yabinoff*! And that is not to mention the other great beauties in my classroom, such as Mist—"

That was the moment when McNally burst in and snatched the microphone from my hands.

"What are you doing?" I wailed. "I need to share my love and joy with the entire school!"

"What are *you* doing?" he growled. "Trying to get me fired? I turn away for a few minutes to try to scare some sense into that Jordan punk, and you do this to me?"

I was startled by the fear in his voice, and knew at once that I had done something terribly wrong. That

knowledge snapped me out of the peanut butter trance and back to reality.

"Oh, McNally," I said. "I fear I have created another incident."

"Yeah," he said. "No kidding. Come on, we're getting out of here!"

When we got back to the embassy, I hurried to my room and locked myself in. Though I knew Tim would not be home yet himself, I fired up the communicator to send him a message.

"Tim," I said, my face and my odors serious. "Please call me as soon as you can. If you can come to the embassy, that would be even better."

I burped twice, made a few knuckle cracks, and then signed off.

I was waiting for Tim when the entry capsule opened. The Veeblax was with me, riding on my shoulder.

"I can see he's been practicing," said Tim.

I glanced to the right and saw that the Veeblax now looked exactly like my head . . . which made me appear to be a two-headed creature.

"Soooo, how do things stand?" Tim asked. "Did your Fatherly One find out about school today?"

"Not yet," I said. "Though I am sure he will before long."

"It wasn't really your fault," said Tim. "Brad gave you that cookie on purpose. And I'm positive Jordan was the one who set him up to do it."

"I figured as much," I said. My face got serious, and the Veeblax imitated my expression. "I called because I want you to help me talk to the Fatherly One about all this."

"Geez, Pleskit. Your Fatherly One is like this inter-planetary big deal. He's not gonna listen to a kid like me. Besides, he's kind of scary."

"How do you think I feel about him?" I asked. "But it is a well-known phenomenon that parental units will accept information from their childling's friends that they will not accept from the childling itself. Please?"

Tim sighed. "He won't vaporize me if he gets mad, will he?"

I shook my head, and the Veeblax copied the gesture. "That would be against the Interplanetary Code of Conduct. Actually, if he does not like the idea that I asked you to speak on my behalf, the one most likely to suffer is me."

"Well, I don't want to get *you* in trouble either," said Tim.

"I am in trouble already. Come on, let's go to the Fatherly One's office to wait for him."

When we reached the office of my parental unit, we were surprised to find no sign of anyone. Not only was the Fatherly One not there, but Ms. Buttsman, Barvgis, and Beezle Whompis were all missing as well.

"They must be having a staff meeting," I said. "We'll go in and wait for him to come back."

"He might not like that," said Tim uneasily. "Remember the last time we went into his office?"

"Well, yes. But that time we were borrowing his Molecule Compactor, which turned out to be a very bad idea. This time we're just going to wait for him. We won't touch anything."

Tim sighed and followed me into the office.

The Fatherly One's command pod floated halfway between the floor and the ceiling. It was empty, and I could tell that Tim was longing to touch it.

"Zgribnick!" I said suddenly. "I just remembered: the Fatherly One does not like me to bring the Veeblax in here. I'd better take him to my room."

"Wait!" cried Tim.

"I'll be right back," I said, turning and walking backward as I spoke. "I need you to stay in case the Fatherly One comes. If he has not already heard about today's events, I want us to be the first to tell him." I turned again and hurried down the corridor.

As I was heading back to the Fatherly One's office to rejoin Tim, I was stopped in the hallway by Ms. Buttsman. "I don't think you should disturb your Fatherly One right now," she said. "He has just received some unexpected visitors."

"But I need to speak to him!"

"It will have to wait. The visitors are from the Interplanetary Trading Federation. Meenom gave strict orders that he is *not* to be interrupted."

"Off-worlders?" I cried.

Lunch Swap Disaster

"They arrived unexpectedly. They appeared to have very serious business."

I stared down the hall, wondering what would happen when my Fatherly One and the off-world visitors discovered an Earth boy in his office.

CHAPTER 14

[TIM]
THE ACCIDENTAL SPY

I looked around Meenom's office. It was filled with fascinating objects.

"I won't touch anything," I muttered to myself. "I won't touch anything. I won't touch anything. I *won't* touch anything."

I repeated the command ten times before I broke down and picked up a strange-looking sphere that kept changing color. As soon as I touched it, a smell like swamp water surrounded me. *Yikes!* I thought, and quickly moved to set the thing back on the counter. Since I am a klutz, I dropped it instead. I watched in horror as it rolled under the counter. I made a quick dive to the floor and began frantically looking for the little thing.

Before I could spot it, I heard voices from the outer offices.

Swinging around on my knees, I saw Meenom standing near the door. He was talking to someone, but I couldn't see who. Waving his hand, Meenom gestured for them to follow him into the inner sanctum.

I scrambled under the counter and pressed myself against the wall. My heart was pounding so hard that I was afraid the aliens would hear it! I just hoped none of them had supersensitive ears!

Even from my hiding place, I could tell that the three beings who entered the office with Meenom were aliens. If their feet hadn't made it clear, their language would have. Cold with fear, I huddled even more tightly against the wall, praying that I wouldn't be discovered.

"Geedrill peedris fli-danji!" said one of the aliens in a voice that did not sound at all friendly.

Meenom burped loudly in response, then made a series of knuckle cracks. An odor that reminded me of a hamster cage that had gone too long without being changed filled the room. Only my terror at being

discovered kept me from gagging out loud. I cupped my hand over my nose and tried to breathe shallowly. That helped, but not much.

A frenzied conversation erupted among the aliens—a virtual symphony of words, farts, belches, and knuckle cracks, accompanied by a series of smells so rich and varied that they made my head spin and my nostrils dizzy, which was not something I would have thought was possible.

What were the aliens talking about? And how angry would they be if they discovered I was listening?

Not that I've understood a single fart of it, I

thought, wishing I had some idea—any idea—of what was going on.

A final burst of words and smells, and then the room fell silent, if not odor-free. To my horror, I saw Meenom's feet heading in my direction. He stopped in front of the shelf under which I was hiding. Speaking softly now, the ambassador picked up something and began to putter with it. As he did, he moved one foot forward.

It nudged against me.

I held my breath.

Meenom dropped the object he had been holding—on purpose, I suspected. Then he bent to pick it up, which brought him face-to-face with me.

I cringed as I saw Meenom's eyes widen in shock and anger. I had pushed myself as far back against the wall as I could, trying to merge myself into it. Now Meenom's purple face and dark eyes seemed to pin me to that spot.

Unable to move, scarcely able to breathe, I mouthed a single word: "Sorry!"

To my astonishment, Meenom stood without speaking.

A moment later, the aliens broke into another babble of conversation.

Feeling slightly less terrified, and driven by curiosity, I slid closer to the edge of my hiding place and peered out.

One of the aliens was clearly from Hevi-Hevi.

Another was tall and slender, with scaly orange skin. This being, whose back was toward me, wore little save a shiny brown shift and a pair of brown shoes that fit so tightly, they looked as if they had been painted on. I looked again and realized I could not tell if they really were shoes, or actually the being's feet. The third alien, who appeared to be female, had an insect-like quality to her features, especially her large, multifaceted eyes. She was waving her four arms and speaking in an angry, buzzing voice.

Meenom had his hands up and was humming a single, soft note, as if trying to calm her. A tangy-sweet odor, something like grapefruit, drifted from his *sphen-gnut-ksher.*

The conversation continued for another four or five minutes, with the insect woman buzzing angrily, Meenom and the other Hevi-Hevian both trying to calm her, and the tall orange being occasionally adding a comment—which it seemed to do mostly by slapping out a rhythm on its skinny, scaly body.

A final, angry buzz from the insect woman was followed by a moment of silence. Then Meenom spoke, mingling words and gaseous eruptions in an oddly musical way. The insect woman buzzed two or three times during his reply, but other than that did not interrupt. When he was done, she lowered her head and flicked out her tongue, which was about three feet long and bright blue. It wrapped around Meenom's wrist, then seemed to pull his hand and her head together. They stood that way for a moment. Then the insect woman withdrew her tongue, shook her head sadly, turned, and left the room. The tall orange alien followed. The third alien—the one from Hevi-Hevi—belched twice, emitted a smell that reminded me of root beer, patted Meenom on the shoulder, and turned to follow the others.

Meenom watched them go without speaking.

After they were gone, he belched a command. The door to the room slid shut. He turned to where I was hiding and said sternly, "You can come out now, Tim."

Bruce Coville

Trying not to tremble, I crawled from beneath the shelf.

"What were you doing down there?" demanded Meenom.

I swallowed nervously. "Pleskit and I were waiting to talk to you. He left for a minute to . . . to do something. When I heard you coming, I freaked out and—"

Meenom raised a hand to stop me. "'Freaked out'?"

"Had a brain spasm," I said. "I thought you might get angry if you found me here by myself, so I hid. I suppose it was stupid, but I was really scared."

Meenom nodded. "I think I understand. My visitors, however, might not have. Having an Earthling here would have been . . . problematic for me. And for your planet. It does look a good deal like spying, you know."

"I'm just a kid!" I said desperately.

"Do you think children have never been used as spies?" asked Meenom, sounding surprised.

"I suppose they have been," I said. Then, feeling a need to get everything out, I added, "I did overhear the conversation. But you were all speaking in alien languages. So it's not like I learned anything."

Meenom laughed. "A good point—though if you

were working for one of my enemies, you could still have recorded the conversation to sell later."

"I wouldn't do something like that!" I cried. "I like you guys. Pleskit is my friend. I would never—"

"Peace, peace," said Meenom, holding out his hands. "I didn't say you did. I just pointed out the possibility." He burped twice and cracked his knuckles. The command pod drifted down to the floor. He stepped into it. "I am well aware that you have been a good, if not always wise, companion for Pleskit."

"I like him," I said. This answer had the double virtue of being true and seeming like a safe thing to say.

"He likes you as well, Tim. In fact, I am a bit envious of the friendship my childling shares with you. I do not have such an Earthling connection—nor am I likely to for some time. My work here is too serious, and too complicated, for me to make myself vulnerable in such a way. Yet such connections are, in the long run, one of the primary pleasures of the work. So it is a relief to speak with an Earthling who does not have a complaint or an economic interest to push." He paused, then said, "Tell me, how do you think Pleskit is adjusting?"

Startled by the question—by the way Meenom was

speaking to me—I wasn't sure how to answer. "Good, I guess," I said at last. "Probably quite a bit better than I would, now that I think about it."

The discussion had made me remember my first experience at summer camp two years earlier, and the desperate homesickness that had gripped me for the first few days. That had been in a place where the land, the sky, the trees, the air, the very beings around me were, if not what I saw every day, at least familiar and safe. As if a curtain had been pulled back, I suddenly had a new sense of what it was like for Pleskit to be here in this totally new place, where nothing was like what he was used to, where everyone he went to school with was of a completely different species. I blinked, stunned by this sudden vision of what my friend had been going through. Looking at Meenom more closely, I asked, "Does he talk about it much?"

"Not as much as I would like. On the other hand, I am not available to him as much as I would like to be. Things right now are . . . difficult."

Feeling bold, and thinking I might never have another chance, I said, "Were those beings that were just here giving you trouble?"

Lunch Swap Disaster

Meenom emitted a smell that reminded me of over-ripe bananas. "They were *messengers* of trouble."

"Do you have a lot of alien visitors?"

"I prefer the term 'off-worlders,'" said Meenom gently. "It's a little less harsh."

"Sorry."

Meenom burped reassuringly. "You don't know unless I tell you. And no, we have not had many off-world visitors. Earth is not on any of the major inter-planetary lanes, so ships do not pass nearby very often. The beings who were just here came out of their way to express their concerns." He closed his eyes for a moment. "There are great forces moving, Tim. I am in a constant state of fret. I must be wise and wary if I am to protect your planet."

"Protect us?"

Meenom looked startled. "Forgive me. I have spo-ken more freely than I should. It is not right to burden you with my concerns. Let us stay with Pleskit. This last . . . episode . . . of his has created new problems with the Trading Federation."

"But it wasn't really his fault," I said, wondering if Meenom had even heard about *today's* problem yet.

Meenom cracked his knuckles and emitted a faint fishy odor. "I wish I could be sure of that. I do not always understand my childling, especially after the events that occurred on our last planet, Geembol Seven."

"What happened there?" I asked. I realized at once that I sounded too eager.

Meenom tapped his nose three times. "I have said too much. I will ask you to keep this conversation in confidence. It might disturb Pleskit to know I was talking to you this way."

"I guess I can do that," I said uneasily. I started to say more but was interrupted by Ms. Buttsman rushing into the room. "Sir, I think you had better come quickly. We've got more trouble!"

CHAPTER 15

[PLESKIT]
GRAND DELUSIONS

I saw Tim and the Fatherly One rush out of the private office but did not give their arrival much attention. That was because I was entirely focused on the alien delegation . . . or, to be more specific, on the insectoid woman who was part of the group. The sight of her strange beauty had triggered whatever peanut butter was lingering in my system, and I had thrown myself to the floor in front of her. Now I was weeping at her feet.

"Don't leave me," I pleaded desperately. "I love the way you click. If you click and I tick, we could make beautiful music together."

Lunch Swap Disaster

"Good grief," I heard Tim mutter. "He's having a peanut butter flashback!"

"Pleskit!" roared my parental unit. "What do you think you're doing?"

"Following my heart, O Fatherly One, just as you have always taught me to do. I have finally found the woman of my dreams, an insectoid whose beauty could make the very planets veer from their courses. I cannot bear to see her simply blast off and leave me!"

The insect woman made a series of angry-sounding clicks and chitters.

"Pleskit, stand up this minute!" roared the Fatherly One. The smell that accompanied his command brought me to my senses. I blinked and leaped to my feet. "Save me from myself!" I cried.

Our visitors all spoke at once, two of them using words that I could not understand. The Fatherly One hurried forward, belching soothingly.

Tim scurried around the group, grabbed my arm, and whispered, "Let's get out of here!"

We hurried to my room.

"I am not fit to live among civilized beings," I groaned.

"That's okay," said Tim, trying to sound cheerful. "At least you'll still fit in here on Earth!"

"There is no humor in this, Tim. I am a walking disgrace, an embarrassment waiting to happen, a social disaster area, a scandal on—"

"All right, all right! I get the picture. But that was just another peanut butter episode, right?"

"I do not know," I groaned. "I do not know anything anymore."

Later that afternoon, the Fatherly One called me into his office.

"What, exactly, is going on with you?" he asked. His voice and the odors emitted by his *sphen-gnut-ksher* were gentle and stern at the same time. "In addition to that outrageous display you put on with our guest from Peablam VI, the school has called to complain of yet another incident."

"I think we have isolated the source of the problem," I said. "I seem to have an extreme reaction to an Earthling food called peanut butter."

The Fatherly One's *sphen-gnut-ksher* sparked— never a good sign. "We are both well aware that new elements in your environment may disturb your metabolism. However, you have been trained from the time of hatching to control yourself better than this, Pleskit. There is too much at stake right now. If you can't keep yourself under control, I fear I will have to withdraw you from the school."

"But, Fatherly One—"

"No more!" he said, raising his hands to cut off my protest. "Please do not add to my already considerable problems."

My insides cold and heavy, I trudged from the office back to my room.

When McNally and I arrived at school on Monday, Mr. Grand again called me to the office.

"Pleskit, your presence here is beginning to affect the other students," he said sadly. "While I am personally fond of you, I cannot let your problems in self-control affect the educational program I am trying to run. I'm sure you understand that this cannot go on."

"I completely agree," I said.

"Good," said Mr. Grand. "So I know you will not take it the wrong way when I tell you that I am going to suggest to your parental unit that he withdraw you from the school, for the good of yourself, the other students, and the developing interplanetary relationship."

"You're throwing me out?" I cried.

Mr. Grand frowned. "That's a very harsh way to phrase it, Pleskit. I am suggesting a voluntary withdrawal, for the sake of all concerned."

"But it's not my—"

"Ah-ah!" said Mr. Grand. "I don't want to hear any excuses. It's time for you to stop blaming your behavior on some imaginary 'chemical reaction' and start accepting responsibility for your own actions. Chemistry only counts in chemistry class."

That afternoon, I asked Tim to come to the embassy with me again.

"I do not know what to do," I said, once we were in the privacy of my room. "The Fatherly One has been called away to urgent meetings, all of which seem to have to do with the disruption I have caused. The good news is, that means he has not yet received Mr. Grand's message asking that I be taken out of school. The bad news is, he will get that message shortly after he returns." I flung myself onto the air mattress, which let me float a few feet above the floor. "I despair, Tim. It seems I bring trouble everywhere I go. If I am expelled, it will be an interplanetary scandal that may end our time here and make Earth subject to colonization!"

"I can't believe Mr. Grand is so clueless!" said Tim. "He's just doing this because you're an alien. If you were an Earth kid, he'd have to go through all kinds of stuff before he could kick you out. You can tell how hard it is to throw a kid out just by the fact that we still have Jordan in our midst." He paused in his rant. "How about McNally? Have you talked to him about this?"

"McNally is in a great deal of trouble too. He let me out of his sight to try to talk some sense into Jordan. But that was a violation of his prime directive. I am terrified that he will be relieved of his duties!"

"That would be horrible!" cried Tim.

"I know. And I feel so guilty about all this. McNally is not blaming me. He says that it was his own fault for trying to deal with Jordan instead of watching me. He also says that if the problem were simply how to attract a girl's interest, he could help me just fine. He seems to feel that is one of his specialties. But on the matter of getting *un*interested in girls, he is of no use."

"Hmmm. We can't count on the Butt for help; she would just as soon have you out of the school anyway. What about Beezle Whompis?"

I looked up in surprise. "I had not thought about him. I do not really know him yet. He is a very strange being."

"Yeah." Tim laughed. "Not normal, like us."

"He does not even have a regular body," I said.

"That might make him all the more suited to discuss bodily functions," said Tim. "He can take an outsider's view on the question."

When we entered the outer office, where Beezle Whompis normally held guard over the Fatherly One's door, we were disappointed to see that the new secretary was not at his desk.

We were turning to go when we heard a crackle of sound. Suddenly Beezle Whompis was there.

"Sorry," he said. "It takes a fair amount of energy to maintain my physical appearance. Sometimes I let it slip when no one is around, just to rest for a bit. Can I help you, Pleskit?"

Lunch Swap Disaster

Quickly I explained what had happened with Mr. Grand at school that day. Beezle Whompis's long, lean face grew dark with anger. He shimmered out of sight and reappeared next to me. "It is not appropriate for a man charged with the education of children to have such a slight understanding of the way chemistry affects the brain, of the way body and mind are linked together. The same kind of thing that happened to you could easily happen to a human, given the right foodstuff."

"You mean you could make humans get all ga-ga-goopy that way?" asked Tim nervously.

"Not necessarily that specific reaction," said Beezle Whompis. "I just mean that you could create a short-term personality change." He peered at Tim more closely. "You look skeptical, young Earthling. Perhaps a demonstration is in order."

"You mean you've got something like that already?" Tim asked.

Beezle Whompis smiled. "Of course not. But I suspect I could work something up without much trouble." He paused for a moment and went frizzy around the edges. Then, as if he had made up his mind about something, he grew solid again and said, "Follow me."

The air crackled as he vanished from sight. A moment later, he reappeared. "Sorry! I keep forgetting that you physical creatures have to travel with your bodies intact. Let's try that again. Follow me."

CHAPTER 16

[TIM]
MONKEYFOOD

Beezle Whompis led us to another level of the embassy, then along a corridor I had not seen before. We came to a door with a plaque that said, in English, RESTRICTED ACCESS: NO EARTHLINGS ALLOWED!

The phrase was repeated—at least, I assumed it was the same phrase—in French, Spanish, and several other languages that I recognized as Earthly but could not name.

Beside the door was something that looked like a keypad. On its surface were fifteen buttons, each of a different color.

I expected Beezle Whompis to tap in a code. Instead

the tall, skeletal alien pointed a single long finger at the keypad.

A crackle of energy shot from his fingertip to the pad.

The door slid open. When Beezle Whompis noticed me hanging back, he laughed and said, "Feel free to enter."

I shook my head. "The sign says 'No Earthlings Allowed.' I don't want to get you in trouble."

Beezle Whompis made a sound like a car trying to start on a freezing-cold morning. (It wasn't until later that I learned this was his way of laughing.) Reaching forward, the energy being tapped me on the head. A jolt of power tingled through me.

"There," said Beezle Whompis. "I have just granted you temporary galactic citizenship." He paused, then added, "Actually, I believe you are the first Earthling to be so honored—at least, by this mission."

"Cool," I said. "Thanks!"

I followed Beezle Whompis and Pleskit into the room. "Cool," I murmured again, dazzled at the sight of all the alien scientific equipment. Two long tables that looked as if they were made of blue glass held everything from bottles and beakers to conglomerations of wire and plastic that were so complicated, it made my eyes hurt to try to figure them out. Viewscreens and monitors lined one wall. I saw three workstations; each had a chair with keypads on the arms and more keypads in front of it.

Beezle Whompis sizzled out of sight and reappeared in one of the chairs. Rather than tapping any of the keys, he placed a finger against a lavender button. For a moment, he seemed to fade. A blue glow flickered around him.

"Ah," he said, unfading as a flood of symbols filled the viewscreen in front of him. "Here we go."

"What is that?" I asked.

"A complete map of the human genome . . . everything you ever wanted to know about your own DNA but didn't know how to ask."

I gulped. "You just have it on file? The government is spending, like, billions of dollars to come up with that information."

"The practice will be good for them," muttered Beezle Whompis, his attention focused on the screen. "Ah, here we go! Hmmm. Oh, *that's* interesting." He began to chuckle, then flickered blue again. The screen changed. "Good," said the energy being softly. "Good. Good. *Aha!* I think we've got it."

He crackled out of sight, then he reappeared again next to the door. "Let's go to the kitchen. I want to see if Shhh-foop can whip up a little recipe for us. Tim, if you're willing to taste it, the results should be . . . amusing."

When we reached the kitchen, we found that Beezle Whompis's "recipe" had already been transferred to Shhh-foop's computer terminal.

"Oh, making this will be lovely fun," she sang, her orange tentacles whirling excitedly. "Sit right down, younglings and Mr. Whompis, and I'll get to work. Would you like a snackie-doodle while you wait?"

"Uh—I think one special food will be enough for me today," I said.

"Alas, alas," warbled Shhh-foop. "Young Earthlings fear the cooking of Shhh-foop. Where is the spirit of adventure? Gone, gone . . ."

Since she sang it more to herself than to me, I didn't feel it was necessary to answer.

Lunch Swap Disaster

"I'd like a bowl of *febril gnurxis*," said Pleskit. Turning to me, he added, "This is my favorite breakfast material, but sometimes I have it for an after-school snack."

Beezle Whompis vanished altogether. When he reappeared, he said, "Having no physical body to nourish, I sustain myself by snacking on energy. Sometimes I go outside to bathe in the sunshine. This time I simply slipped into the embassy's circuits for a little electron soup, so to speak."

"Ready!" sang Shhh-foop a few minutes later. She slid over to the table, holding a silvery tray. On the tray were a stack of crackers (or something that looked like crackers), a spreader, and a bowl of goo. The goo looked a little like peanut butter, or at least like peanut butter would look if it were purple, not quite as thick, and given to releasing an occasional bubble, like a glass of soda working in slow motion. Or a mini volcano popping lava.

To my surprise, the stuff *smelled* amazingly good.

"What is it?" I asked.

Beezle Whompis smiled. "Try it and see."

"I haven't had real good luck with alien food," I said nervously, remembering the explosive aftereffects of the *finnikle-pokta* I had eaten the first time I'd visited the embassy.

"Ah, but I designed this to be compatible with the human digestive system," said Beezle Whompis.

I took a deep breath, then reached forward and spread some of the purple goo onto one of the cracker things.

The smell was so delicious that I was actually eager to eat it.

I took a bite, then chewed for a minute. "S'good!" I cried, popping the rest of the cracker into my mouth. "*Very* good!"

I spread another and ate it. Beezle Whompis stopped me as I was reaching for the third.

"Let's wait and see what happens," he said.

I looked longingly at the bowl of goo. "Okay," I sighed. "But I want Shhh-foop to give that recipe to my mom."

"I rather doubt your mother will want this one," said Beezle Whompis.

I started to answer. Before I could get the words

out of my mouth, my eyes went wide. I twitched twice.

"Oook!" I said, scratching under my arm. "OOO-OO-O-OOK!"

Then I leaped from my chair. Bending over, I pressed my hands against the floor like an extra pair of feet and went scrambling out of the room.

CHAPTER 17

[PLESKIT]
MONKEY BUSINESS

"Ai-yi-yikkle-demonga!" wailed Shhh-foop, forgetting, for the first time since the embassy had landed, the Fatherly One's rule about speaking only in the language of our host country.

Beezle Whompis crackled out of sight. I sprinted down the hall after Tim, wondering if the Fatherly One's new assistant was a traitor like Mikta-makta-mookta after all.

I found Tim leaping up and down on top of Ms. Buttsman's desk, chanting, "Ook! Ook!" as he flung papers into the air.

Ms. Buttsman was crouched beneath the desk, shrieking for help.

"Tim!" I cried sternly. "Tim, get down from there!"

"AAAAIIEEEE!" shrieked Ms. Buttsman, which didn't really help things much.

"Oook!" said Tim. Then he vaulted off the desk and raced across the room, where he began trying to climb one of the embassy's *moizel* plants. The plant's large purple leaves whirled wildly as it tried to defend itself from the intruder. It was just reaching out with a wiry purple vine when Tim leaped away and onto one of the seating devices.

I took several deep breaths, trying to keep myself from slipping into *kleptra*. Ms. Buttsman peered over the edge of her desk and shrieked again.

At that moment Beezle Whompis crackled into view. "This way, McNally," he called behind him. "Hurry!"

An instant later, McNally appeared at the door to the room.

"Oook! Oook!" squealed Tim.

McNally heaved a deep sigh and strode to the seating device where Tim was hunched. "Tim, get down from there!" he said sharply.

Tim leaped forward, landed on McNally's shoulder, and then scrambled over him and leaped to the floor. With another "Oook!" he headed for the door.

McNally made a flying tackle and caught him just before he left the room.

"Well," said Beezle Whompis triumphantly. "I guess that proves the point!"

"Oook!" shrieked Tim.

"Do you have an antidote?" I asked nervously.

"Only time," said Beezle Whompis. "Another ten minutes or so and he should be fine."

"Easy for you to say," growled McNally, who was struggling to keep Tim from crawling away. "What did you do to the kid, anyway?"

"Merely gave him a little monkeyfood," said Beezle Whompis, sounding so innocent, it was actually possible to believe he didn't see anything wrong with the idea.

"What," demanded Ms. Buttsman, crawling out from under her desk, "are you talking about?" She began fussing with her hair.

"Just a small experiment, dear lady," said Beezle Whompis, causing Ms. Buttsman to sniff in disdain. "We wanted to see if we could create a reaction in Tim similar to what peanut butter causes in Pleskit. The substance we came up with stimulated what your scientists sometimes refer to as 'the lizard brain,' causing Tim to revert to a primitive, apelike behavior that lies hidden as a latent possibility in every human."

Ms. Buttsman snorted. "Given that boy's typical behavior, I don't think getting him to act like an ape represents any great scientific breakthrough."

"I believe the ambassador prefers the staff to not say insulting things about our host species," replied Beezle Whompis.

Ms. Buttsman snorted again and started to gather the papers Tim had strewn about. "I'll thank you to remove him until . . . until whatever it is you did wears off," she said. Her voice was so cold, you could have cut up the words and used them in a drink.

Beezle Whompis nodded to McNally, who managed to pick up the still-*ooki*ng Tim and carry him from the room.

Beezle Whompis's prediction turned out to be correct. In ten minutes' time, Tim reverted to his normal self. Blinking, he looked at McNally and said, "Why are you holding me?"

Lunch Swap Disaster

"Let *them* explain," growled McNally. "I'm supposed to be on break right now!" Letting go of Tim, he began brushing off his clothes. "Will he be all right now?" he asked Beezle Whompis.

"He should be fine."

"Good. Next time you try an experiment like this, you might tie him down first. Or at least do it while I'm not taking my nap."

Shaking his head, he left the room.

I quickly explained to Tim what had happened after he'd eaten the substance Shhh-foop had prepared.

"Wow!" said Tim. "It really is monkeyfood! Now Mr. Grand will have to believe us!"

Mr. Grand, of course, did no such thing. When we went to see him the next day, he listened to our story with growing impatience.

"A fine concoction," he said when we were finished. He began pacing back and forth in front of us with his hands clasped behind his back. "If you boys were doing this for a creative writing project, I would expect you to get a good grade. But you don't need to be telling *me* this kind of fairy tale. I don't believe in such nonsense. People control their own destinies, and there is no sense blaming their actions on chemicals. That is the coward's way out—all excuses and no accountability. A real man takes responsibility for his actions."

When we told this to Mrs. Vanderhof, she was outraged on our behalf.

"I can't believe that man is so obdurate!" she fumed, setting a plate of chocolate chip cookies on the table. "Of course people should be responsible for their own behavior. But it's not always possible. He's so stuck on that one idea that he's ignoring reality!"

I glanced at the cookies. "Do these have any peanut butter in them?" I asked nervously.

Mrs. Vanderhof looked offended. Then her face relaxed. "You're smart to be cautious, dear. But no, there's no peanut butter in them. I made them for the PTA Welcome Back event tonight." She smiled. "I figured I ought to have you three sample them first—to make sure they're good enough."

"Good figuring!" said Tim enthusiastically.

Still feeling a little nervous, I picked up a cookie

and took a big bite. *"Skeegil sprixis!"* I cried. "These are wonderful!"

Mrs. Vanderhof smiled modestly. The smile faded as her thoughts returned to Mr. Grand. "That man makes me so angry! Even if he doesn't trust my experience—or yours, Pleskit—he really ought to know that three kids in your class are taking medication to control their behavior."

"They are?" asked Linnsy.

Mrs. Vanderhof nodded. "Some prescriptions help certain people focus better. Kids who have trouble concentrating can find it helps their behavior in school considerably."

"Who's taking it?" asked Tim eagerly.

Mrs. Vanderhof shook her head. "That's not my story to tell. You know I believe in being completely open about what I've experienced, Tim. But I also believe other people have to make that decision for themselves. The point is, your principal has proof right in his classrooms of the way body chemistry affects behavior, and he should be aware of it."

"Proof or not, he's still threatening to ask Meenom to pull Pleskit out of school," said Tim bitterly.

"He hasn't done it already?" asked Mrs. Vanderhof.

"The Fatherly One is not always easy to get in touch with," I explained. "He has been dealing with emergencies for the last couple of days. But he is coming home this evening, and I fear he may want to go to the PTA reception. If he does, Mr. Grand will almost certainly talk to him while he's there, since he knows he may not get another chance right away."

"Then we have to do something tonight," said Linnsy. "It's our last chance!"

"Do *what*?" I asked.

She shrugged. "I don't know. A demonstration or something. Prove to Grand the monkeyfood does what you said. Then he'll have to accept the idea that the peanut butter could have caused your troubles."

Tim put down his cookie and sighed. "Well, I guess there's no way around it. I'm going to have to make a monkey out of myself again—this time in public!"

CHAPTER 18

[TIM]

OPERATION MONKEYFOOD

The Parent-Teacher Association usually held its annual Welcome Back Night earlier in the school year. But the disruption—and security problems— caused by having the world's first alien in atten- dance had caused the group to move the date back to mid-October.

Some parents grumbled about the armed guards, and having to come through two sets of scanners before being allowed into the school. Others said they thought *every* school should have such an elaborate security system. Others were grumpy about the pro- testers, who were still standing just outside the police lines, and shouting anti-alien slogans at the people who were allowed in.

Because Mom had been scheduled for a late shift at the hospital where she works, and hadn't been able to get out of it, I came with Linnsy and her parents. Given what I was planning to do that night, this was just as well, as far as I was concerned.

"Well, doesn't this look nice!" said Mrs. Vanderhof when we came in.

The cafeteria had been decorated with artwork from most of the classes. A big WELCOME BACK banner made by the fourth graders stretched across the back wall.

I looked around, wondering if Pleskit had arrived yet. I didn't need to wonder. The moment he did show up at the door, the whispers started.

"Look, there he is!"

"It's the alien boy!"

"Holy cow, he really *is* purple!"

Parents who had not yet had a chance to see Pleskit in person were elbowing to get near him. Everywhere people were craning their necks to see the world's most famous sixth grader.

Lunch Swap Disaster

It took me several minutes to work my way through the crowd to my friend's side, and I had to step on a fair number of toes in the process.

"Have you got the goo?" I whispered when I finally reached him.

"Right here," said Pleskit, patting the pocket of his robe.

"Then Operation Monkey is under way!" I said.

Only it wasn't, really. As we watched for our opportunity, we realized the flaw in our plan: Mr. Grand was spending almost all his time talking to the adults, and wasn't going to be particularly interested in talking to any kids—particularly kids he viewed as trouble—on this occasion.

"Now what do we do?" I muttered.

"Let's try standing by the food table," suggested Pleskit. "I've noticed that Mr. Grand has what you call a 'sweet tooth.' He's bound to come that way sooner or later."

"What are you two plotting now?" asked McNally when he saw us whispering.

"Just going for cookies," said Pleskit. "Want to come?"

"As if I had a choice," muttered McNally. "Stand back, everyone!" he bellowed. "Coming through. Give the kid some air."

I was astonished at how much easier it was to move through the room with McNally in the lead.

Mrs. Vanderhof was standing behind the food table, smiling and chatting as she poured glasses of punch and helped people find just the right cookie. "Any luck, boys?" she asked when she saw Pleskit and me standing in front of her.

"Not so far," I said glumly.

"We thought if we waited here, we might have a better chance of talking to him," said Pleskit.

"Good plan," said Linnsy. She had just come out of the kitchen with a new platter of cookies. "Mr. Grand always chows down hard at these things."

"These two all right with you for a minute, ma'am?" asked McNally.

"Of course," said Mrs. Vanderhof with a smile.

"All right, don't move," said McNally to Pleskit. "I'll be back in a flash."

He poured two glasses of punch, and began to

make his way through the crowd again. To my surprise, he was heading for Ms. Weintraub. I was even more surprised by the way our teacher smiled when McNally handed her the glass of punch. But before I had time to think about that, I saw Mr. Grand coming toward us.

My throat got dry. Somehow I found the idea of speaking to the principal—who was already unhappy with me—far more unnerving than any of the very real dangers Pleskit and I had faced since we'd first met.

When Mr. Grand was nearly at the table, I said, "Could I have a word with you, sir? It's about Pleskit."

Mr. Grand frowned. "This is not the time for anything like that, Tim. Come see me tomorrow."

"But tomorrow will be . . ."

I didn't bother to finish the sentence. Mr. Grand had turned and left.

"This isn't going to work after all!" I groaned. "He's not going to give us a chance!"

"On Hevi-Hevi," replied Pleskit, "we say, 'If the *pawpreet* won't come to the *skrizzle*, the *skrizzle* must go to the *pawpreet*.'"

"What the heck does that mean?"

Pleskit pointed to the front of the room, where

a microphone had been set on the stage for short speeches from Mr. Grand and the PTA officers.

I gulped. Even though I had been ready to make a fool of myself in public in order to help Pleskit, I hadn't counted on doing it *onstage*.

"If Mr. Grand's request that I be pulled from the school reaches the Fatherly One, the humiliation will be unbearable," said Pleskit. "However, my deepest worry is not for myself. My fear is that if he sends a formal request for my withdrawal to the embassy, it will have to be passed on to higher levels. That could be deadly for the Fatherly One's mission!"

I remembered what Pleskit had told me about the possibility of Earth being colonized if his Fatherly One lost the franchise. The idea was horrifying. "Give me the monkeyfood," I said. "I have a duty to the planet!"

After taking the container from Pleskit's outstretched hand, I made my way toward the front of the cafeteria. As I got closer to the stage, my stomach got tighter and tighter.

What am I doing? part of my brain was shrieking.

It was getting two answers. One section of my brain was boldly saying, *You are saving Meenom's mission,*

helping your friend, and protecting the entire planet.
Another, milder part of my brain was saying, *What are you doing? I'll tell you what. Making an incredible fool of yourself, that's what you're doing!*

I hated making a fool of myself. On the other hand, I was used to it.

And the stakes were high.

A set of six steps led up to the stage. I started up them.

CHAPTER 19

[PLESKIT]
A SWINGING PARTY

At first only a few people noticed Tim, since almost everyone was busy in conversation.

He stepped up to the microphone, tapped it to make sure it was on, and then said, "Ladies and gentlemen!"

Conversations began to die down. Heads turned in his direction. Some people looked puzzled, but it was obvious that most of them thought this was part of the program.

I looked around at the sea of faces and was horrified to see Jordan Lynch and Brad Kent standing near the edge of the stage. I hadn't even thought about them being here.

Lunch Swap Disaster

Too late to turn back now, I thought as Tim tightened his grip on the microphone stand. I knew this was hard for him, and it warmed my *smorgle* to know that I had such a good friend.

Tim continued. "As some of you may know, my friend Pleskit has had some . . . uh . . . problems of a romantic nature recently."

Everyone turned to look at me.

"The thing is, all that wasn't really Pleskit's fault. See, it turns out he has this, like, allergy to peanut butter, and when he eats it, it just makes him go all goopily romantic and start spouting the most ridiculous and gooey love talk."

You don't have to help that much, I thought.

Just then I saw Mr. Grand pushing his way through the crowd. He had a furious look on his face.

Tim began to talk faster. "The problem is, some people don't really believe that's what was happening. Some people insist that blood chemistry can't affect your behavior at all. So we needed to give you some proof." He held up the jar of monkeyfood. "Here it is. This is a food we cooked up over at the embassy. I'm going to eat some now, and you'll see how it causes me to act like a monkey."

"That's enough, Tim!" shouted Mr. Grand. He was almost at the stage now.

Tim tried to open the monkeyfood. To my horror, the top wouldn't come off the container!

Mr. Grand was at the edge of the stage.

"The bottom!" I shouted from the far side of the room. "Tim, push on the bottom!"

Tim heard me and did as I said. At once, the top of the container popped open. He was about to stick his finger in and take a swipe of the goo, when Mr. Grand snatched the container from his hand.

"Tim, how foolish do you think I am?" he said angrily. "You can eat this food and then pretend to act like a monkey, and what does it prove? Nothing but that you wanted to act like a monkey."

"He acts like a monkey anyway!" shouted Jordan, who was obviously enjoying this.

"Quiet!" snapped Mr. Grand. "Now, look, this is utter nonsense, and I'm going to prove it once and for all."

With that, the principal stuck one finger into the container, took out a big gob of purple goo, and then stuck his finger into his mouth and licked it off.

Lunch Swap Disaster

"There!" he said. "Now, if there were anything at all to this nonsense you've been spout—"

Mr. Grand stopped. He clutched at his throat. His face twitched. His eyes went wide.

"Oook!" he cried, bending forward and scratching himself under his arm. "Oook! Oook!"

Most people in the cafeteria looked baffled. A few, assuming it was some sort of skit, began to laugh. Others looked frightened.

"Aoooga!" cried Mr. Grand, pounding his chest and stomping across the stage. "A-*oooo*-ga!"

Now people began to look really nervous. Someone screamed. Several parents grabbed their kids and ran for the exits. A few ran without their kids. I saw Jordan, who I had always suspected was a coward, scramble under one of the tables.

"Aoooga!" cried Mr. Grand again. He grabbed the microphone and began snorting into it, then shrieked and pounded the microphone against the floor.

Mr. Philgrinn, the gym teacher, rushed toward the stage. Five of the fathers joined him.

Seeing them coming, Mr. Grand leaped across the stage, grabbed the edge of the curtain, and began to

climb. When he reached the top, he flung himself over their heads onto one of the cafeteria tables.

"Aoooga!" he cried, pounding his chest. "Aoooga!"

Three more parents—two mothers and a father—tried to grab him.

Flexing his legs, he leaped straight up and grabbed one of the support beams that stretch across the cafeteria ceiling. Swinging from beam to beam, he began making his way toward the refreshment tables.

Shrieking people scrambled to get out of his way.

He landed on the end of the table—the *very* end, which made it act like a huge lever.

Mr. Grand's end of the table went down.

The other end went up.

Cookies, cakes, and cups of punch soared across the room.

That was when McNally made a flying tackle and dropped Mr. Grand.

I wasn't sure whether to laugh or run for my life.

Then I looked to the side of the room and saw the Fatherly One standing in the cafeteria doorway.

Running had definitely been the right answer.

Unfortunately, it was too late for that.

CHAPTER 20

[T I M]
FINAL TEST

Pleskit's Fatherly One was not happy. He had been not happy when he'd nabbed us at the PTA reception. He had been not happy during the drive back to the embassy in the limousine. And he had been not happy as he'd led us to his office.

Now, pacing back and forth in front of his command pod, he was still not happy.

"That was totally irresponsible," he fumed. His *sphen-gnut-ksher* was emitting the smell of disapproval, which reminded me of insect repellent with a slight overtone of burritos.

"It was also totally undignified," said Ms. Buttsman.

Lunch Swap Disaster

"Thank you for your input, Ms. Buttsman," said Meenom. "Would you please fetch Mr. McNally for me?"

Ms. Buttsman gave us a sour look but went to do as asked.

Once she had gone from the room, Meenom said, "Now, much as I disapprove of what you did, I must admit that you got your point across rather clearly. I have already received a call from Mr. Grand saying that if we will fully explain to the press what prompted his eruption of monkey behavior tonight, he will withdraw his objections to Pleskit's remaining at the school, take any reference to past problems out of your permanent record, and replace them with a note saying you should not be allowed to consume peanut butter in any form, as it affects your brain chemistry."

He paused, then added, "I fear I did not give you sufficient credit for your story of what had happened to you, Pleskit. You have my apology."

Pleskit nodded. "Accepted, O Fatherly One."

Meenom raised an eyebrow, made a clicking sound at the corner of his mouth, and emitted a smell like lemon juice. "Don't get carried away. You're still in plenty of trouble. As are you, Timothy."

I blushed and felt nervous.

"We will determine what discipline you will receive later," said Meenom. "Tim's, of course, will come from his own parental unit. Right now, however, I wish to move on to other matters—namely, the issue of peanut butter. Do we have any in the embassy?"

"I do not believe so, Fatherly One."

"Actually, we do," said McNally, who had just entered the room. "I keep a jar myself. For snacking purposes, you know."

"Would you bring me some, Mr. McNally? I would like to conduct a brief experiment."

McNally raised an eyebrow, then shrugged and said, "Be right back."

Pleskit and I watched eagerly as Meenom opened the jar of peanut butter, held it beneath his nose, and sniffed.

"Divine aroma," he said. Then he dipped one long, purple finger into the peanut butter, took out a good-size dollop, and popped it into his mouth. "Mmmm! A strange taste, but most excellent. You say this is a common food on your planet, Tim?"

Lunch Swap Disaster

"I eat it every day."

At that moment Ms. Buttsman entered the room. "Sir, I have a message for you from—"

She broke off as Meenom leaped to his feet, crying, "Ms. Buttsman! Has anyone ever told you what a glorious creature you are? Your existence must be a joy to the cosmos, for you bring delight wherever you go!"

"Boy, and I thought *you* said some ridiculous things when you ate peanut butter!" I whispered to Pleskit.

Ms. Buttsman looked confused. Then her face twisted in an odd way. It took me a moment to realize that she was smiling. Even more startling, it was a pleasant smile. Who knew she could do that?

"Why, Ambassador Meenom," she murmured. "What a lovely thing to say!" Looking confused, she backed out of the room. "I'll come back later," she said as she closed the door.

Meenom blinked, shook his head, and took a deep breath. He stared at the jar of peanut butter in wonder.

Then he began to laugh.

"What?" cried Pleskit. "What is so funny, O Fatherly One?"

"This is it!" said Meenom, his *sphen-gnut-ksher* emitting a floral scent. "Our first export, Pleskit! We can sell tons of this stuff on Hevi-Hevi. We'll call it 'Return to Romance.' It will be a public service—when used in the appropriate situations, of course!"

Bowing to us, he said, "My thanks to you both. You have saved the mission!"

And the planet with it, I thought happily.

CHAPTER 21

[PLESKIT]
A LETTER HOME (TRANSLATION)

FROM: Pleskit Meenom, on the always-interesting Planet Earth
TO: Maktel Geebrit, on the much-missed Planet Hevi-Hevi

Dear Maktel:

Well, that's it—the story of the strange new substance that you'll probably be hearing about as soon as the sales campaign is ready. I hope Hevi-Hevi is ready for all that romance!

The Fatherly One and I have discussed the new export in some detail. He says that civilization requires the control of our own urges, which in many situations means understanding and conquering our own chemistry. But to conquer chemistry, we must first acknowledge it. If we pretend it does not count, then we can never deal with the reality of how it affects us.

Anyway, I hope you enjoyed hearing about my latest problem. I will confess that I did not put in *all* my secret feelings. Oh, I was completely honest. But there were a couple of things I kept to myself as I worked on this with Tim, mostly because I have learned that Earthlings are often uncomfortable talking about emotions. I didn't say anything about how homesick I get, for example, or how strange this world seems to me from day to day as I try to get used to it. I didn't talk about how I long for the familiar sights and smells of Hevi-Hevi. I didn't put in that sometimes I feel so far from home that it is like a big lump has grown in my *clinkus* and I can hardly move.

Lunch Swap Disaster

It's not as if I am totally alone. I have been making friends here. I have the Fatherly One, and the Grandfatherly One. Most of all, I have Tim. I didn't really talk about how much I truly like Tim—or about the fact that I sometimes worry that he only wants to "hang out" with me (as the Earthlings say) because he is so interested in everything alien.

On the other hand, if I think about that too much, we can never be real friends.

The Fatherly One always says, "Trust, but verify." Sometimes, though, I think you just have to trust.

The Fatherly One also says that whenever two cultures meet, there are always ways in which they clash. How they deal with the collision of ideas and beliefs is part of forming the relationship, and a test of a culture's maturity.

The Earthlings have so little idea of what is waiting for them out in the wider universe. But as I grow more and more fond of them, as I start to feel more at home here, I hope more and more that the Fatherly One's mission will succeed. Partly for our sake, of course; after all, it would be nice to be rich.

But even more for the sake of the Earthlings.

Do you think it will really work out for you to visit, Maktel? I am very excited by the possibility. (If I can just keep from getting thrown off the planet before you get here. . . .)

Please write soon.

Fremmix Bleeblom!

Your pal,

Pleskit

SPECIAL BONUS:

On the following pages is Part Four of "Disaster on Geembol Seven"—Pleskit's story of what happened on the last planet where he lived before coming to Earth.

This story is being told in six installments, one at the end of each of the first six books of the Sixth-Grade Alien series.

The next thrilling chapter will appear in Book Five, *Zombies of the Science Fair!*

DISASTER ON GEEMBOL SEVEN

PART FOUR:
CITY OF THE CONSTRUCTS

FROM: Pleskit Meenom, on Planet Earth
TO: Maktel Geebrit, on Planet Hevi-Hevi
Dear Maktel:

We now come to the difficult part of what happened on Geembol Seven.

As you will remember, I had been on the planet only a few days when the Fatherly One took me to the Moondance Celebration, where I spotted a six-eyed boy named Derrvan who clearly needed help. But it was a trap, of sorts, for when I followed him to the waterfront, I was pulled into a hidden elevator that took me (and Derrvan) down to a secret cavern.

Balteeri, the being who pulled me in, was a "construct"—an illegal combination of biological and mechanical parts. He and Derrvan wanted me to hear their story. I agreed, despite their warning that to listen was a crime. But before they could even begin, construct hunters burst through the wall of the cave. To escape we went deeper into the planet, where Balteeri had a flying ship. After a harrowing trip through rocky tunnels, we came at last to a most amazing place.

The cavern that opened below us was lit by dimly glowing spheres that floated about forty or fifty feet above its stony floor. I tried to count, but soon realized there were several hundred of the things. By their gentle light, we could see that there was a small city nestled below them.

As we drew closer, I realized with horror that it was a city of constructs. That is, everyone I saw walking its streets was like Balteeri: a strange combination of natural and mechanical parts. Knowing that such creations are illegal, it had been startling enough to see Balteeri. To see an entire city filled with such beings was a real *clinkus* tightener.

Balteeri brought our ship to a gentle landing at the edge of the city. One of the glowballs floated over to hover directly above us, making it easier to walk to the city. Since the path we followed was twisty and littered with stones, I appreciated the light.

"Why have you brought me here?" I asked as we walked.

"We were being chased," snapped Balteeri. "Or have you forgotten that already?"

"How will I get back?" I asked, not caring if I sounded self-centered.

Balteeri set his jaw. "That remains to be seen."

Derrvan had said nothing since we'd landed. I glanced at him. He was staring ahead of us with a hungry expression, as if this were something he had been looking for, longing for, all his life. "This is my father's city," he whispered when he saw me looking at him.

"Was your father a construct?"

I asked the question timidly, not sure whether it would be offensive.

"His father was the savior of the constructs," said Balteeri grimly. "Which is what cost him his life. Now come along."

Ignoring my desire to ask more questions, he started forward. Derrvan and I followed, lagging just a few feet behind. "Do not mind Balteeri," he whispered. "He is gruff, but he has a good spirit."

Yes, but is it real or mechanical? I wondered. It was not a question I dared to ask out loud.

I had already lived on three different planets, so I was used to being surrounded by beings who were unlike me in appearance. But never had I felt so different, so out of place, as I did in the city of the constructs, where Derrvan and I appeared to be the only beings made entirely of flesh and blood.

Lunch Swap Disaster

All around us on the narrow streets were half-natural, half-mechanical creatures like Balteeri. Yet each was unique; each had his, her, or its own special combination of added parts, extra arms or legs or tails, usually with cleverly designed tools attached. Some were actually mounted on wheels and didn't walk at all. Some had most of their birth faces, with only small patches of metal or plastic; others had heads that were nearly all constructed and would have seemed robotic except for the look in their eyes.

They stared at Derrvan and me oddly as we passed. Some seemed angry, some almost hungry; some seemed to flinch at the sight of our unaltered, fully natural faces and bodies. I was struggling not to flinch myself, torn between my basic training about accepting difference and all the evil things I had heard about constructs.

"Where are we going?" asked Derrvan, after we had been walking for several minutes.

"You'll see soon enough," replied Balteeri gruffly.

Only a moment later he led us down a side street. We passed a tavern where raucous singing and laughter flowed from the open windows—an unexpected bit of warmth in this strange place. The street was quieter after that. It came to a dead end in front of a small but very beautiful building.

Without bothering to knock or ring a bell, Balteeri opened the door and stepped in. Derrvan and I followed.

"This looks like a chapel!" I exclaimed.

My surprise must have sounded in my voice, because Balteeri turned to me and said angrily, "I suppose you think that just because we're half-mechanical, we have no souls."

"I hadn't thought about it at all," I said honestly. "I just wasn't expecting you to bring us to such a place."

He nodded silently, but I got the impression he found my answer acceptable. Before any of us could speak again, we heard a voice from the far end of the chapel ask, "Is someone there?" Before we could answer, the same voice cried joyfully, "*Balteeri!* You've come back. Do you have good news for us?"

Balteeri closed his eyes, and the biological half of his face looked pained. "I have but a slender thread of hope, Serha Dombalt. Nothing more."

"That is more than we have had so far," replied the *serha*, moving into the light.

Serha Dombalt wore a hooded robe of silvery blue, cinched around the waist with a black cord. The hood was up, hiding much of her face. Even so, I could see that she was a construct, not only from the glint of metallic skin that shone from beneath the robe but from the fact that one of her six-fingered hands was covered by light green flesh, while the other was made of metal and capped by fingers that each had a different mechanical design and function.

She seemed startled by the sight of Derrvan and me. "You've brought *two* organics with you," she said. In her voice I could hear curiosity, fear, and even a hint of accusation.

"This is Derrvan, whom I first went to seek," replied Balteeri. "The other is Pleskit Meenom, childling of the new ambassador from Hevi-Hevi. Derrvan and I intended only to seek his help, not bring him here. But we were pursued—"

"Are you sure you weren't followed here?" interrupted Serha Dombalt. "You could put us all in the gravest danger—"

"We are already in grave danger," replied Balteeri, his voice unexpectedly gentle. "That was the point of all this."

Serha Dombalt bowed her head. "Forgive me, Balteeri," she whispered. "It is an old reaction, and deeply ingrained."

Balteeri waved her apology aside. "The point is, as long as I have the ambassador's childling here, it makes more sense for you to tell him our story. You know it more directly than I do. Besides, you're nicer than I am. The boy may be willing to hear things from you that he would resist from me."

Serha Dombalt nodded, then drew back her hood. "Come with me," she said.

Swallowing, trying to ignore the burst of fear and revulsion I felt at the sight of her half-organic, half-mechanical head, I walked with Derrvan and Balteeri to the front of the chapel, where Serha Dombalt led us around a speaker's stand to a narrow doorway covered by a metallic blue curtain.

We went down three steps into a small, cozy room that appeared to have been carved directly into the stone. Serha Dombalt gestured for us to sit on a long stone shelf. (Fortunately, it was covered by thick padding.)

She gazed at me intently. Her organic eye showed sorrow and compassion; her mechanical eye was cold and unblinking. "So," she said. "You are the slender vessel in which all our hopes reside."

Lunch Swap Disaster

"I do not understand! What is it you want of me?"

She closed her eyes and whispered, "We want you to save us from complete and utter destruction."

To be continued ...

A GLOSSARY OF ALIEN TERMS

Following are definitions for alien words and phrases that appear for the first time in this book. While most are from Hevi-Hevi, you will find a few from other alien tongues as well. (Note: definitions for alien words that first appeared in Books One, Two, and Three of Sixth-Grade Alien can be found in Books Two and Three of the series.)

The number after a definition indicates the chapter where the term first appears.

For most words, we are only giving the spelling. In actual usage, many would, of course, be accompanied by smells and/or body sounds.

AI-YI-YIKKLE-DEMONGA: The literal translation of this is "Run for your life—someone's been sucking the crazy fruit again!" However, over time it has come to be used as an all-purpose expression of fear or concern.

(Shhh–foop, by the way, is not speaking Hevi–Hevian here, but in her excitement has reverted to the language of her own world, Mirdop 2. Interestingly, "Ai–yi–yi!" as an expression of concern or fright appears in at least 419 different languages.) (17)

BEEZLEDORF: A being whose heart–head ratio is out of balance, and who therefore lets emotions rule thoughts. (Literally, a "soft thinker.") The opposite extreme is a *dartdorf*—a thought-ruled being who has forgotten the importance of emotion and feelings. (9)

GEEDRILL PEEDRIS FLI–DANJI: "You are pampering these creatures!" (Not Hevi–Hevian.) (14)

KILGADDURR: Important site in Hevi–Hevian mythology. In brief, all the forces were in place for an enormous battle that would have cost tens of thousands of lives, when a character called "the *sheelkirk*" (see below), beloved for her grace and beauty, made a sacrifice that so stunned the four armies involved that the battle was canceled. The moment is considered the beginning of true civilization on Hevi–Hevi. (13)

PAK–SKWARDLES: A high-protein, slightly sweet Hevi–Hevian snack made from fermented *dweezil* beans that have been stored in a cool, dark place for at least three months. (7)

PAWPREET: Half of a biological unit found in the southern wampfields of Hevi-Hevi; incomplete without a *skrizzle. Pawpreets* and *skrizzles* are notorious for their stubbornness, and if they are separated, there is a fifty-fifty chance they will die before either will make a move to reconnect. It is only the ones that will overcome their tragic stubbornness that survive. (18)

SERHA: A being who has given its life to studying matters of the spirit; also used as a term of respect for any being considered to be particularly wise. (serial episode)

SHEELKIRK, THE: A tragic, semidivine character in the first Hevi-Hevian epic poem; one of the most beloved characters in Hevi-Hevian mythology. (13)

SKEEGIL SPRIXIS: Literally, "Now has joy returned to me!" An all-purpose exclamation of delight coined by the poet Brigdingle the Strange. (17)

SKIBWEE: A hairy purple flower found in the northern wampfields; particularly loved for its delicate beauty and intoxicating (literally) aroma. (13)

SKRIZZLE: The dominant half of a biological unit found in the southern wampfields of Hevi-Hevi; a hard-shelled creature with a soft underbelly. (See *pawpreet.*) (18)

SQUIBOODLIAN: A popular stuffed toy particularly beloved by Hevi-Hevian children; by extension, a term of endearment between sweethearts. (3)

ZGRIBNICK: A word used to express distress; the equivalent of "drat" or "phooey." (11)

What if everything you drew came true?

From Sid Fleischman Humor Award–winning author of
Milo: Sticky Notes and Brain Freeze

Max is about to face the scariest place he's ever been— South Ridge Middle School!

EBOOK EDITIONS ALSO AVAILABLE

ALADDIN
SIMONANDSCHUSTER.COM/KIDS | MAXCRUMBLY.COM

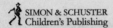